Loves Epiphany

A Novel Written By: Navarro Love

NAVARIA

ENTERPRIZES

NAVARIA ENTERPRISES

Navaria Productions
Copyright © 2021 Navaria Enterprises
Registered, WGAw No. 2106464

ISBN: 978-0692223543
Navaria Enterprises/Navaria Productions and the "Ne" logo are trademarks belonging to Navaria Enterprises.

PRINTED IN THE UNITED STATES OF AMERICA

Navaria Productions

NavariaEnterprises@gmail.com

"The purpose of art is washing the dust of daily life off our souls" –
Pablo Picasso

"No great artist sees things as they really are. If he did, he would cease to
be an artist"
-Oscar Wilde

"If art is to nourish the root of our culture, society must set the artist free
to follow his vision wherever it takes him" – JFK

"The world is but a canvas to our imagination" – H.D. Thoreau

EPIPHANY: A sudden manifestation of the essence or meaning of something.

When life is personified through love and love through music, the mystery of the two can be found hidden within the keys of a piano. When played the sweetest sound of Love and Life become reality, manifested through melody.

Dedication

"For those who understand love is without obligation, this is my gift to you."- Navarro Love

Introduction

What's in a dream? A simple word, but for many it means so much. For others it's just a term to describe those things we've come to reflect upon only when our bodies come to rest. For many it is to vision of those things we long for, or those things long past that we hope to have once more.

A dream, by definition, carries three meanings. Dream, a series of thoughts, visions, or feelings that happen during sleep. Dream, an idea or vision that is created in your imagination, and that is not real. Last, a dream, something that you have wanted very much to do, be, or have, for a very long time.

If your dream is an accomplishment. Something you've wanted to do, be, or have for a very long time. Does it ever come to pass? Do we chase that dream forever as we never stop dreaming, imagining, being, wanting? In life sometimes one will be asked if they have accomplished anything. What have they done that will be remembered? I submit that life itself is a dream and should be remembered not for its accomplishments, but for the sake of the journey one takes to navigate the road of life.

We all live in order to expire. The dream of existence being everlasting life, written and documented throughout time as a prize all should strive to attain. Though the thought of death is one of a morbid and very depressing nature, it is in fact a part of life. In many cases one can look back on their life and see many struggles to which they successfully overcame and through it all they continue to live, chasing that one thing that validates their existence.

Validation can and should be found in the one thing that we most often take for granted, but it is our most beautiful accomplishment day in and day out. That one thing we do without strife, fear, heartache, jealousy, envy, pain, or the many trappings that life itself can bring due to our shortcomings.

Forget all those things that we think validate our life or our dreams. Being successful in life is based upon the nature and state of mind. What one thinks is happiness, may not be happiness to the next. As I often say, money can't buy you happiness, but it will pay for the search. Yet, the search is within. At what price is your happiness? Is it for sale?

Try something simple. Sometimes success can be very simple. Living life can be as simple as breathing air. Success, as some would suggest, is a form of productivity. Fulfilling the dream is a matter of exhausting energy to accomplish a goal. Again, I submit that life is the goal and the steps to accomplishing that goal, attaining that dream are as simple as breathing air. Life becomes so simple when we just choose to breathe.

The next time you are asked if you have accomplished anything in life, your response should be "yes I have". As I am often asked, what is my greatest accomplishment? My accomplishment in life is that I breathe and that I have lived. There is no greater accomplishment than that. I celebrate life with breathing. Slowly taking in the gift accepting its nourishment and expelling the pieces of me no longer needed to exist.

The greatest gift of life is breathing. Throughout the dream, always remember to breathe…

Loves Epiphany

A Novel Written By: Navarro Love

Navaria Productions

1

Nightmares

A COOL AUTUMN NIGHT, all is calm. Not even the sound of crickets penetrates the calm brought by the cooling winds on this fall night in suburban Chicago.

Though the night is as calm as the oceans still waters, all is not calm inside the home of one ten-year old little boy. Navarro, a very shy ten-years-old, is not interested in things most ten-year old's are. He possesses a mind developed well beyond his years. Some would say he has an old soul trapped within a small frame.

He lies asleep in bed while the rumbling of an argument ensues in the living room between his mother Karen, a beautiful slender 30-year-old woman with flowing black hair and her drunken abusive boyfriend Wayne, a very domineering and fear imposing man. Nights like this have become commonplace in the household. So much that with the rumbling and rage building outside his room, it has not yet wakened Navarro.

Suddenly Navarro's eyes are opened by his bedroom door exploding open by the force of a body being thrown against it. He awakes his eyes wide open witnessing his mother slamming down on the bed beside him frantic, crying and screaming. Wayne follows into the room with dots of blood spattered on his t-shirt and scratches around his neck.

Karen, with her nose dripping with blood quickly moves across the bed to create distance between her and this man who has nothing but anger and rage in his eyes. She screams out to him "Stop! Please, stop! I'm sorry." Wayne rushes toward her. "I told you, stay out of my fucking wallet! I will fucking kill you. Do you understand?" Foaming at the mouth he moves closer to her, like a rabid dog moving in closer to a wounded animal. "Your issues are not my problem!" he says. His voice crashes like thunder against her ears. Each word shaking the bones within her body sending chills throughout her frame. She trembles in fear.

Wayne comes closer to Karen as if to hit her again. She franticly moves closer to Navarro anticipating the blow to come. Suddenly Navarro jumps on top of her shielding her with his body, yelling out half in anger and half in fear. He screams!

"Don't touch my mommy! Leave her alone!" Stunned by Navarro's action Wayne is taken back as if for a second realizing what he has just done in front of this small ten-year-old boy. He looks down at the both of them as they are cradled together, Karen whimpering grasping Navarro close to her chest.

Wayne stares at the both of them for a moment then looks down at an empty wallet he's holding, to his belief the cause of the argument. He then turns and walks slowly out of the room slamming the door behind him. Navarro turns to his mother with tears in his eyes.

"Mommy" he says softly. "Are you okay, Mommy?" Karen visibly shaken and bruised grabs Navarro and hugs him tightly around the neck. The strength and bond between the two grow stronger as it becomes apparent that he is her only lifeline. She takes a moment to gather herself strengthening her voice as if to console him.

"Baby I love you." she says stroking his cheek. "You are all the man I need, my big strong man." Mustering the strength, she gives him a smile in order to ease his fears and those or her own.

She then kisses him on his forehead and gives him a strong embrace, one that would take the breath out of anyone, but this embrace breathes life into the both of them. He kisses her back and gently wipes her tears away. "I love you too mommy." He calmly whispers. The two of them exhale and lie down one next to the other. They embrace ever so tightly while silently saying to one another "The storm is over now. I've got you".

2

A New Day

THE MORNING BRINGS LIGHT OF A NEW DAY. The previous night has become so common it's like it never happened. As Karen drives Navarro to school the ride is consumed with silence. The only sound of wind beneath the car and noise of traffic outside the car windows still does not penetrate the noticeable silence within.

Neither having much to say all the while knowing what the other is thinking they sit staring out of the car windows. The culmination of so many nights erupting in violence at home has made them both numb. Numb not only to the feeling that something is completely wrong, but also numb to what a healthy life and existence should look and feel like.

They both sit in silence content with letting the sounds of the road and the radio drown out the ambition of what is building inside of them.

As they pull up to the school kids of all ages are running around in many different directions trying to beat the early morning bell for class. Karen turns and looks at Navarro. He is visibly upset and doesn't want to leave the comfort of being under his mothers' arms. She motions toward him and out of nowhere the silence is broken.

"Baby I know things seem bad right now but...." taking a moment to breathe. "We are going to be okay. I'm going to be okay. We just have to make this work baby. Things will be okay." Navarro doesn't say a word he just nods his head. Choking down the emotion within him he moves closer to her as she wraps her arms around him. They embrace for what seems like an eternity interrupted by the sound of the school bell ringing signaling class is about to start.

Karen reaches over to push open Navarro's door. His mother so close to him he can smell the sweet and loving smell of her perfume from her neck. He breathes her in before collecting his things to exit the car.

"Hurry before you're late." She says to him directing him out of the car. "I will be here when you get out baby. Have a good day okay."

Navarro gets out of the car and walks halfway down the sidewalk leading to the front door of the school building. He stops, turns back to look at his mom. He gathers himself and all the strength he can out of his small 4-foot 10-inch frame.

"I love you mommy". He states boldly, as if he is comforting her with his words.

Karen's eyes begin to water after seeing this, she blows him and kiss and mouths the words back to him. "I love you."

Navarro waves to her as she drives away. He pauses for a second to collect himself before he enters the school building. The school grounds have become still and quiet as all the other kids have gone inside. Navarro looks around for a moment, thinking to himself "should I go in"?

He walks up the few stairs to the front door of the school. He takes a deep breath before opening the door. He walks inside and disappears into the building as the big steel schoolhouse doors close behind him.

Outside Karen drives a few blocks before the intense feeling of sorrow and pain comes full circle. She pulls to a stop sign and rests her head on the steering wheel of the car breaking down in uncontrollable tears. She screams out to God, "Please help me!"

"Please tell me what to do."

She searches for answers to relieve the stress and pain of what she is dealing with at home and more so how to make it better for her son. "God" she begs. "Please help me and please don't let Navarro hate me for not being strong enough."

Her tears flow stronger, then abruptly she is interrupted by the sound of a car horn behind her. Someone yells from behind "Hurry up, move!" In a rush she gathers her thoughts, wipes her face, and drives on.

As the morning passes Navarro finds it hard to keep his attention on the teacher as he stares out of the classroom window daydreaming. He watches as the leaves of autumn dance across the schoolyard. A beautiful blend of colors creating a masterful scene of bliss and serenity in his mind, far from the harsh reality that awaits him at home. The leaves dance, moving back and forth across the pavement. One after the other they race from one side to another leaping from the ground as if they were ballerinas dancing to an orchestrated play.

Suddenly his sanctuary, that is his mind, is interrupted by the sound of a woman's voice calling his name. It is his teacher who has been calling for his attention for quite some time. "Navarro, Navarro, Navarro!" She grows angrier each time she calls to him.

Navarro quickly turns to the teacher with a blank look on his face. The teacher directs him to look at the black board.

"Do you know the answer to the problem?" she asks pointing to the blackboard.

Navarro looks at the math problem the teacher has drawn on the black board behind her. A series of numbers are written on the board. The teacher, pointing to the black board asks. "Do you know the answer? 2 times 25 plus 25 equals what?"

Navarro looks at the problem then looks around at the class that at this point has begun to giggle to themselves. He pauses for a second and looks around the room again. The giggles grow into laughter as the teacher tries to gain control of the class.

"Class quiet down! Quiet down." She says. She then redirects her attention to Navarro. "Navarro do you have the answer?" she asks again.

Navarro looks at the teacher for a second then turns to look out of the window. Silence travels throughout the room. The teacher becoming impatient at this point asks all the students for the answer. In frustration she asks, "Okay does anyone else have the answer?" Melanie, one of the little girls sitting in the front row of the class raises her hand.

"I know the answer."

"Okay Melanie, what is the answer." The teacher replies. Before Melanie can answer a voice resonates from the back of the room.

"75" Proclaiming softly.

The teacher asks, "Who said that?" The class turns; all attention is directed at Navarro, as he sits still looking out of the window.

"Navarro was that you?" The teacher asks.

The class grows even quieter, all attention drawn to Navarro. He turns and looks at the teacher, pauses for a second, then responds confidently.

"The answer is 75."

The teacher in shock pauses for a moment before responding. "Okay um, yes, yes that's correct. Nice job Navarro." She says congratulating him.

The class that had just finished mocking him with laughter all sits in amazement that he answered the question and actually spoke. The teacher directs everyone's attention to the front of the room as she begins to draw out another problem. The class turns and looks at the black board, all with the exception of one curious little girl. Melanie stays fixed on Navarro, something churning within her, sparking her curiosity. She sits and stares at him for what seemed like several seconds. After a moment he notices and looks back at her. As they make eye contact, she gives him a smile and waves. He gives way to a slight smile but does not wave back before glancing once again out of the window to watch the dancing leaves on the school grounds.

3

A New Friend

ITS TIME FOR LUNCH and all the kids are in line in the hallway leading to the cafeteria. As the kids flow down the hall, they walk past the music room. As Navarro walks past, he hears the sound of someone playing the piano. The sound grows stronger as he gets closer. He becomes drawn to it, each step he it grows stronger and stronger.

The sound of Mozart fills the room. Navarro stops as he peeks into the doorway. Afraid he leans in slowly. His body half in the hall the order in the doorway peering in to hear more of this sound. As his eyes scan the room, he finds someone there.

Sitting alone at the piano is the music teacher getting ready for his next class. He doesn't notice Navarro as he continues to play, with each note it grows more compelling, each sound more vibrant than the first.

Navarro stands hypnotized as he listens to a sound he has never come to know before. The background noise of children laughing and at play is drowned out by the sound of Mozart's "Piano Concerto in E FLAT".

Navarro stands lost in the music being played; suddenly with a tap on his shoulder he is awakened from his daze, its Melanie. She is trying to get his attention by forcefully shaking his arm.

"Navarro, Navarro. What's wrong?" she asks with a look of innocent concern.

He turns to her as he comes to life out of his daydream. "What is it?" he asks as if he has no idea he was just in a trance.

Her voice sounding as sweet as a bird's song asks of him "Do you want to sit with me at lunch?" Navarro pauses and thinks for a second before answering with the only word he can muster. "Okay".

Melanie smiles the biggest smile then grabs Navarro by his hand and leads him to the cafeteria. The thought of making a new friend has come secondary to the sound of the piano still ringing blissfully in his ear. A feeling he has never felt comes over him as he quickly walks away with Melanie his head turns searching to hear that sound again.

As time goes by and the day draws to an end, Navarro has survived another grueling day of stares and laughter but today he didn't have to struggle through it alone. On this day he made a new friend.

After school Navarro and Melanie are standing outside talking as parents are pulling in to pick up their kids from school. They stand in silence, of course Navarro not being one to begin a conversation watches as other kids are running around in all directions smiling and laughing as their parents are greeting them, while putting them in the car to leave.

Melanie grows tired of the silence and begins to inquire about Navarro. As all kids do with questions, she doesn't hold back what comes to her head. Abruptly she asks. " So, who is coming to pick you up today?"

"My mom." Navarro replies in voice devoid of any feeling.

"You really don't talk much do you?" Melanie questions in a more up-front manner. Navarro turns to her. Eager to say something, but he turns away and places his head down as if his tongue is tied.

"Well its okay, you don't have to talk that much for me. We can still be friends if you want." Navarro looks long and hard at Melanie as if an unbearable weight has been lifted from his chest. He pauses before responding. "Okay, I want to be your friend too."
Just as the two share a smile Melanie's parents arrive. They honk the horn to call her over to the car.

"Well that's my dad, I have to go. Um, now that we're friends, we can sit together tomorrow if you want." She says.

Navarro giving way to a slight smile wants to say so much, but he cane only find one word to express himself. He replies with an internally emphatic and eager "Okay."

Melanie runs quickly toward her father's car, but yells back to Navarro before getting in the back seat. "Well, I will see you later tomorrow. Bye"

Navarro waves back holding a smile on his face eagerly awaiting tomorrow. As he looks around sitting alone that old feeling begins to come back. That feeling of being alone once again comes over him. His moment of having a friend, someone his age interested in him has come to a swift end as Melanie has left him. He waves goodbye to Melanie as he watches her climb in the back seat of her father's car. She turns to him and rolls down the window giving him a big smile, waving as her parents pull off.

At that moment Navarro's mother pulls up in her car and honks the horn for him to come over. He runs to the car with a big smile on his face as if he hasn't seen her in days. She opens the car door as he jumps in. They embrace for a moment as she then directs him to close the door before driving away.

During the drive, Navarro looks down at his mother noticing she has on her nurse's work uniform. He thinks to himself for a moment that if she's going to work, he has to stay home with Wayne. The idea of that is totally uninviting to him and very scary.

Karen, noticing that he is watching her tries to lighten the mood. "So how was your day baby? She asks. "I see you made a new friend".

Navarro, not taking the bait instantly responds. "Ma, why do you have your uniform on?"

Karen becomes irritated by the question.

"Baby, we've been through this. You know I work some evenings. I know you don't like it but that's how it is right now. Okay?"

Navarro turns his head to look out the window. He doesn't say a word, just knowing what could possibly be waiting for him at home is enough to turn his little stomach inside out.

The long drive comes to an end as they arrive at home. Karen pulls the car to the curb and stops. Before getting out of the car Navarro turns to his mother to make one last plea before going into the house.

"Momma, I don't want you to go." He says, with his little heart pounding against his chest. "Well, baby I have to. I will see you when I get off okay? I need you to be good for me baby." She says placing her hand on the back of his head kissing his forehead.

"Yes ma'am." He replies softly. He doesn't want to go against his mother's wishes, but he can't help but to be apprehensive about going in alone knowing Wayne may be waiting for him. Karen tries to comfort him and make him feel better about being home alone but instead she confirms his worst fear.

"Things will be okay baby. I will be home soon. Wayne is home. So, just try to be a good boy okay?"

Navarro frozen with fear doesn't say a word he just nods his head.

"Okay now go baby" Karen rushes him out of the car, "I will see you when I get off, then maybe you can tell me about the new friend you made."

Navarro hesitantly replies, "okay", before reaching for the door handle.

Karen leans in and hugs him, "I love you baby." She whispers to him. Navarro doesn't say a word he just grabs a tight hold on her not wanting to let go. After a moment he pulls back and moves toward the car door again.

He gets out of the car and waves to his mother as she drives away. Once again, he finds himself standing alone on a long sidewalk wishing that his mother were there to walk with him. He turns and heads toward the front door. He tries to keep his spirits up as he enters the house knowing that this could possibly be a very long night.

4

He Stands Alone

NAVARRO STANDS ALONE with his back to the door surveying the living room. It's unusually quiet he hears nothing. It's as if he's the only one there. Still he stands in silence knowing that at any moment Wayne could appear. Suddenly a slight sound from the back room of the house catches his attention.

He walks down the long hallway leading from the living room to the back bedroom, peeking around every corner as he goes. He focuses on every step walking slowly as he goes, not making a sound as he steps one foot in front of the other.

As he walks closer and closer to the back bedroom the sound grows louder. He is aware that Wayne is in the back room, but he is curious as to what Wayne is doing. He curiosity in many ways overcomes his fear as he moves in closer. He passes the hall closet suddenly there's a sound. The bedroom door swings opens.

Nervous Navarro quickly jumps into the hallway closet to hide. The door opens Wayne appears, staggering and tripping over himself in a rush to the bathroom. Navarro watches through the crack in the closet door.

His heart begins to beat against his chest, not in fear but in growing curiosity as to what is going on. He has no idea of what he is witnessing, but curiosity is taking control of him. He watches as Wayne goes in the bathroom. He waits for a second until he hears the bathroom door lock. Quickly he jumps out of the closet and steps over to the bathroom door. He puts his ear to the door and hears the sound of Wayne vomiting.

Even more curious than before he wonders what is going on with Wayne that has him running to the bathroom with such urgency.

Navarro turns away from the bathroom door and looks toward the bedroom. He thinks for a moment, "Should I, or shouldn't I walk in." He fights the urge to do so but he is so caught up with wanting to know what has just happened he can't help himself.

He walks into the room, the door creeks, and his heart stops. Thinking Wayne has heard the sound. He rethinks whether he should go in, but he has come this far he isn't about to turn back now. He surveys the room quickly with his eyes and in the corner the nightstand grabs his attention. He moves a little closer to the nightstand as he does, he notice's something sitting atop the nightstand with smoke coming from it.

Once he reaches the nightstand he stops and wonders what he is looking at. He sees a small cylindrical glass pipe with what appears to be burn marks on it. Next to it sits a lighter and a foil wrapper. He reaches down and picks up the glass pipe and examines it with his eyes. Suddenly the door crashes open with a loud boom. It's Wayne! Screaming and fuming.

"Boy what the fuck are you doing! Put that shit down! Get the fuck out of here!"

Navarro almost pee's his pants he is so scared. Wayne charges him and grabs him by his arm making him drop the glass pipe he was holding. It shatters on the floor. This only infuriates Wayne more.

He screams at Navarro, "You fucking broke my shit!"

"You little bastard. Who told you to come in here?"

He begins shaking Navarro vigorously, and slapping him across his head. His blows are so hard Navarro goes in and out of conscientiousness. All he can do is go limp and close his eyes in hopes that it will be over soon. Wayne grows even angrier that Navarro doesn't respond to him.

"Answer me boy! What the fuck are you doing in here?" He screams.

Navarro is so in shock he can't say a word. Wayne growing madder by the second takes him by the arm and leads him out of the bedroom toward the hallway. He drags Navarro out to the hallway and opens the closet door. With no regard or remorse, he throws him down on the closet floor. Navarro's little body bounces off the cold hardwood floor as he lands in the corner. Wayne feeling ten feet tall looks down on Navarro. Snickering he says.

"Maybe some time in here will teach you to open your fucking mouth. You little shit!" Navarro looks up at Wayne as he slams the closet door. The last remaining pieces of light are snatched away as the door is slammed shut and locked.

Navarro cries out from the closet, " "No! Let me out! Let me out!

"Mommy! Help me! Help me mommy!"

Wayne bangs on the door and yells equally as loud.

"Shut the hell up! You'll fucking come out when I say you can."

Wayne walks back to the bedroom and begins to pick up the pieces to his crack pipe. Navarro cries out once more, and then takes notice that help isn't going to come. He closes his eyes and settles himself in the corner of the closet. He closes his eyes and clutches his knees to his chest as he begins rocking back and forth comforting himself.

His cries turn to sniffles, his sniffles to quick short breaths. As he regains control of himself, he slowly starts to accept the fact that the closet he was once hiding in is now his prison. The only comfort is that of peace and quiet, yet what kind of peace can be found in solitary confinement with no light and only the cold floor to keep you company.

Minutes turn to hours and hours seem like an eternity as he sits there waiting for someone, anyone to save him from this dark cramped cell. Tired and beaten he falls asleep, apparent the only thing he can do to escape this nightmare is to dream himself to another place. Total darkness, no sound, no light. The only comfort - piece of mind ones-self.

Stuck in a dream like state he sits alone, waiting. Waiting for an answer to a long-spoken prayer, to be rescued from the horror of his home life. Hard to imagine a child wanting to die just to escape the trauma of not being loved, not being seen as a blessing but yet being regarded as a punching bag to what he sees as the evilest of men.

Yet he waits. He waits for an answer. He waits for God's hand to come down and save him from this cold dank closet corner. He waits alone.

Hours come and go, as Navarro lay asleep. Without any warning suddenly the closet door bursts open, and arms reach in to grab him. He is awakened and startled by this. Afraid he begins to fight, swinging his arms in all directions trying to hit anything that comes close to him.

"No, No, No, leave me alone stop! Leave me alone!" He screams.
He swings at the darkness with his eyes tightly closed shut. Suddenly a familiar voice calls out to him.

"Baby it's me. Its mommy baby. Shhh, stop baby stop. It's me"

Navarro relaxes and almost instantly faints in Karen's arms. She picks him up and carries him off to bedroom. With his weakened voice Navarro says to her, "I needed you mommy." Cradling him in her arms she tries to comfort him.

"I know baby. I'm here now. Its okay I'm here now. Let's go to bed."

Navarro clutches her around the neck tightly recalling what he just went through he pleads to her. "He tried to hurt me mommy, I needed you, I needed you"

She tries to comfort and calm him, holding him tightly in her arms she says, "Don't worry about him baby. He can't hurt you now, I'm here now, I've got you now."

Karen carries Navarro into his bedroom and places him down on the bed. She undresses him and places him under the covers. She whispers to him.

"Go to sleep now okay. Have sweet dreams for me. I love you baby. I'm here and I won't let anything happen to you." Karen kisses him on his forehead before leaving the room. She walks toward the door before exiting she turns to Navarro once more and whispers, "I love you."

She looks at him for a moment before turning out the light. She pulls the door slightly closed, leaving it open just enough to let the light from the hallway pass into his room.

Karen walks into the back bedroom where Wayne is waiting for her. Immediately upon entering the room he slams the door shut behind her and an argument ensues. The sounds of which wakes Navarro. He opens his eyes startled for a moment. He lies still on his back. Listening to the sound of two voices one louder than the other. Yelling back and forth followed by the sound of bumping against the walls. Knowing that there's nothing he can do he rolls over in the bed curls up into a ball and begins to cry. He closes his eyes and begins to wish himself away from his present state. Again, his wishes are unfulfilled so he can do nothing but lie there motionless until sleep finds him again.

The midnight hour draws near, and the turmoil of hours past have come to a still calm. Navarro, in bed asleep is awakened to sounds of his mothers' voice. The sound, though it is faint, sounds as if she is crying. Navarro listens for a while then gathers the strength to crawl out of bed and walk toward the hallway leading to the back bedroom.

He peeks through a crack in his door and notices a light coming from under his mothers' bedroom door. He walks slowly to the back, watching his every step uncertain whether or not Wayne will jump out at any given moment.

As he walks down the long cold hallway the sound gets louder. One voice turns into two voices. And crying gives way to a distant moan something his ears have never heard before. As he reaches the door, he can see that it is cracked. Just a little yet enough for him to peek inside. What he witnesses sends the feeling of a splinter piercing his heart. He sees Wayne on top of his mother thrusting his body against hers. He watches for a moment then notices the look of ultimate bliss on her face. Confusion gives way to disappointment, heart-wrenching disappointment. The site brings him to feel like she has betrayed him. He was sure that after what Wayne has done, she would finally take him away from the abusive ways of this man. But alas, it is not going to happen.

Navarro turns his back to the bedroom door and walks halfway down the hall before propping himself against the wall. After a moment of standing his legs give way and he slowly slides down the wall coming to rest on the cold hardwood floor.

Thoughts racing through his head give way to doubt. He slowly begins to question whether his mother even loves him at all. How can she enjoy being with this man after what he has done? How can she give so much of herself to this man, a man that hates her son, her little boy? Those thoughts and still he can't ignore the noises filling the air around him. It becomes too much for him to handle, at this moment he closes his heart to everything. He tells himself that nothing matters at this point not even life itself. He gets up from the floor, walks to his room, and closes the door behind him. Accepting the point of fact that he is truly alone.

5

The Morning After

THERE IS TENSION IN THE AIR as Karen fixes breakfast. She's in a rush to get Navarro dressed and ready for school before she has to set out for work. From the kitchen she yells out to him, "Navarro, come to breakfast. Hurry up honey your going to be late."

Wayne in another room hears the noise and commotion coming from the kitchen staggers in yawning and scratching his head in an attempt to wake himself up. "What's all this damn noise? I'm trying to sleep." Karen pleads in a frustrated tone, "Wayne don't start please."

"Start what I'm trying to sleep." He replies with much attitude.

He walks over to Karen. He grabs her from behind wrapping his arms around her waist aggressively kissing her on her neck. Playfully he confesses. "Oh, I'm sorry baby. You know I'm just playing."

"Stop I have to go to work." She begs becoming more frustrated with his attempts and the thought of being late for work again due not only to his advances, but also the effort taken to get herself and her son ready for their day.

Confused Wayne grabs her tighter, "Stop? You weren't saying that last night, now were you?"

Karen tries to push him away again, with this effort raising her voice slightly. "Come on now stop. I have to go." Wayne gets upset that she is not interested in his advances and that she is pushing him away. He grabs her aggressively around her arm and pulls her close to him. So, close she wrenches as their noses almost touch. Looking her directly in her eyes he says to her.

"Don't tell me what you have to do! I don't give a fuck!" He becomes more physical and aggressive with her. Pulling her closer to him as Karen pulls equally in the opposite direction. Wayne leans over and forcefully kisses her and at that moment they notice Navarro standing in the doorway. Wayne stops and releases Karen as she scrambles to collect herself. She moves a few steps away from Wayne and motions to Navarro to sit down at the table.

"Come on baby. Come eat before we have to go." She says.

Wayne gives a look of disgust and contentment to Navarro. He yells out at him,

"Yeah come sit down and eat damn!"

Wayne snatches a chair from under the table and sits down. Navarro just stands there and looks at him for a moment. So many things rushing through his head, thing's he wants to say but doesn't. Words cannot express the level of hatred and disdain filling his heart and soul for this man.

Within his heart and mind, he's tired of running, tired of being afraid. Wayne yells at him again. "Did you hear what I said? Sit down and eat."

Navarro ignoring Wayne turns to his mother and shifts subjects.

"Mommy, aren't you taking me to school?" He asks. Karen still a little shook tries to address his question as composed as she can.

"No baby I can't. I have to be at work and I'm already late. You're riding the bus today. But I will be there to pick you up after school." She says.

Navarro doesn't say a word. It's obvious that this has upset him as well as the many other disappointments he's been subject to in the last 24 hours. He looks at his mother then Wayne before jumping out of his chair rushing out of the house to wait on the bus. Wayne cracks a sinister smile before yelling out him. "Where the hell are you going? Come back here and sit down."

Karen shows her frustration by smacking Wayne hard across the arm. Defiantly she tells him. "Stop talking to him like that." Before she even realizes what, she has just done an infuriated Wayne jumps from his seat and slaps her hard across her cheek.

"Don't ever put your fucking hands on me!" He warns pointing his finger at her.

He thrusts his finger to her forehead pressing her head against the kitchen counter. All she can do is whimper in hopes that he will not hit her again.

"Okay, okay I'm sorry." She whispers in fright.

Wayne backs away from her allowing her a little distance. He stares her down for a moment before giving her a smirk as if to say, "*I thought so*". Karen shaken for a moment gathers herself then runs out of the kitchen chasing after Navarro. She rushes through the living room making her way to the front door. She peeks out of the glass window on the door before opening it. She takes a moment to compose herself before stepping out on the front porch. Outside she sees Navarro sitting there, waiting.

Navarro sits on the bottom steps of the porch waiting on the bus to pull up. He sits hoping the bus will come soon to take him away from the storm brewing inside his home. After a moment of silence Karen moves closer to him and sits on the step behind him. She makes and effort to connect with him not wanting him to go to school without first saying goodbye. She speaks softly behind him.

"Penny for your thoughts."

Navarro ignores her. He stares out at the street searching for the bus with his eyes. Karen moves even closer to him leaning down putting her lips next to his ears she repeats.

"Penny for your thoughts"

Navarro unfazed still glances out at the road. Karen tries again this time she nudges him, touching her knee to his. Navarro can't hold his feelings in anymore. He takes her up on the chance to share his thoughts.

"Mommy why are we here? Why can't we leave, just you and me living together? He asks. "I hate it here."

"Baby I know. There are just some things you don't understand." She says.

Navarro quickly responds back. "I do understand. I understand a lot momma. I hate him I hate it here. I wish we never lived here." A blank look comes across Karen's face. "Don't say that baby." She says.

"Its true, I hate him, and I hate it here." He screams back at her.

Navarro becomes increasingly more upset. This is the moment he has been waiting for. The moment he can express himself freely about all that he feels and how he hates the situation his mother has put both of them in. Unfortunately, his anger and contempt are directed at his mother. All that he feels and all that he holds within him has come to a boiling point.

"Baby things are just temporary, things will change." Karen tries to explain but to no avail.

Navarro is frustrated and fed up. He's tired of hoping and wishing that things would change for the both of them. He questions his mother like he has never done before.

"When mommy? When will things change? You told me that before, but when?"

Karen moves down to the step that Navarro is sitting on. She sits closer to him and looks him in the eye. "Baby I know. I promise things are going to change. You just don't understand Wayne. I know he doesn't show it sometimes, but he loves me, and you. I make him mad sometimes and I know I shouldn't. But he loves me, and I love him. And you know that I love you"

At that moment the bus pulls in front of the house. Navarro gathers his book bag and stands in front of his mother on the steps. With a solemn look on his face he looks her square in the eye and says to her, "Sometimes I think you love him more than me." Karen shows a flustered look as if she doesn't know why he would say something like that to her.

"Baby don't ever say that." Pulling him closer to her. "I love you more than my heart can hold. Don't ever think that I don't love you. Do you understand?"

Navarro pulls back away from her. He doesn't want to hear it anymore.

"Then why don't you show me more? Why do you let him hurt me?" He asks. His face dripping with tears, he turns and runs to the bus. Karen jumps up from the steps and motions after him. Navarro quickly makes his way up the steep stairs into the bus as Karen reaches out to him. She stares watching as the bus doors close behind him. Trying but with no hope of holding back, her tears begin to flow. She watches as Navarro sits in his seat and stares out the window to her. She reaches out to him mouthing the words *"I love you"*, as she watches the bus pull away. Slowly the bus makes its way down the street and disappears. Karen tries to collect herself before walking up the stairs to the front door.

Before opening the door, she turns and looks down the street once more, thinking to herself that her one and only reason for living has just rolled away on a bus for school. What she has just heard resonates within her sending a thumping pain through her chest leaving her heart broken. She immediately breaks down and falls to her knees crying. She folds over grabbing her stomach holding herself tightly around her arms and shoulders. Her tears flow uncontrollably as she has finally realized that the one thing that is most important to her doesn't realize that he is in-fact loved by his mother.

She sits there for a moment bringing herself under control. She gets herself together and stands to her feet. She now realizes something must be done. She must do more for herself and for her son. She reaches out to the front door to go inside. She wipes her face and composes herself before stepping inside.

As she enters the house the door slams behind her, her heart jumps out of her chest as the sound of the door slamming rings out like a gunshot. She turns around frightened by the loud crash and sees the image of Wayne standing behind her with a ferocious look on his face.

Karen sees the rage in his eyes and grows more frightened. He grabs her and throws her to the ground. Charging her he kicks her in her ribs sending excruciating pain through her side. All she can do is curl up and grab her ribs, screaming out in pain. Wayne charges in again. "Don't ever talk to me like that again bitch!" Karen scrambles on the floor and reaches the kitchen. Wayne follows screaming louder and louder, drowning out her cries. She screams at him. "Please no! Stop, please stop!"

Wayne follows her along the floor grabbing at her ankles. "Where the fuck do you think you're going? Come here!" He grabs her leg pounding his fist deep into her thigh while cursing at her. "You want to scream and talk shit to me huh? I'll give you something to scream about." With each word he hits her harder and harder bruising and swelling her inner thigh.

Karen tries once again to get away from him. She wiggles her leg away from him and scrambles faster toward the kitchen. She finally reaches the kitchen and jumps to her feet. She searches the kitchen counter and sink looking for something to fight him back with. Soon after Wayne appears again. With tears in her eyes, her hair a mess and bruising on her thigh and ribs she says in a defiant tone.

"Leave me alone, I swear I will kill you!"

Wayne rushes Karen as she fumbles to pick up a knife from the counter to fight him off. Wayne struggles to gain control of Karen as she fights back swinging the knife at him. She cuts him slightly on his forearm.

He pauses for a moment to assess the damage to his arm and his ego. He can't believe she actually cut him. He grows even more infuriated by this. He lunges at her again. Her strength is no match for his, as he overpowers her. Karen pulls together the last bit of strength she has and lunges back at Wayne. They struggle for a moment but alas her strength is no match for his he quickly overpowers her. He wrestles the knife away from her and throws it to the ground. He hits her with a backhand that rattles her teeth and snaps her head back. He grabs her to stand her up for another blow to her stomach.

He clinches his fist drawing his hand back he thrusts his fist into her stomach sending an unbearable pain through her body. She immediately falls to her knees clutching her stomach unable to say a word. He comes for her again. He draws his hand back, balling his fist up tight and throws a blow to her face that drops her head to the floor. In an instant her body goes limp. He stands over her to witness what he has done. Breathing heavy and bleeding he takes a moment to gather himself and again look at the cut on his arm.

His ego and arrogance once again take hold of him as he straightens his shirt and screams down at her. "See what you made me do? This shit was your fault." Karen lies still beneath him. Still enraged Wayne takes another opportunity to strike. He lifts his foot as high as his knee will go then drops down on her chest crashing into her sternum.

He pauses for a moment before walking out of the room. He turns looks at her and even after he has beaten and humiliated her to no end, he goes even lower by spitting on her. Karen can do nothing but lay there bleeding and moaning with pain.

6

His Passion

THE MORNING RIDE to school is just like any other. It's
bumpy and long. All the kids screaming and yelling all in fun
while Navarro sits in his seat staring out of the window. He sits
there watching the houses pass by one after the other. He watches
as the cars pass one by one, all the while hoping that the bus will
not stop at the school but take him to a place far away from here.

Navarro's anger becomes so imbedded within him he
grows colder inside. As the bus moves on, the passing of buildings
one after the other brings calm within him. Navarro leans back in
his seat, closes his eyes, and thinks of the day he first heard the
sound of peace in the form of a piano. As if he had written the
piece, he remembers each melody as it plays in his head. Note after
note he recalls what he heard.

It begins soft with a low volume. The music consumes his thoughts, each note growing louder and more vibrant than the first. Navarro lets himself go within the music as it plays in his head. The sounds of the kids on the bus become muted the road noise goes silent. All he hears are the notes one by one resonating in his mind.

He envisions himself sitting there playing the piano vigorously hitting the keys pounding out the notes, creating a perfect marriage of melody and chords. He becomes intoxicated by the sound of music flowing through his mind. He begins to sweat uncontrollably. Over and over the notes become clearer and more vibrant. His heart pounds equally as vibrant. He heart soon becomes in lock step with the sound of the piano. As if his heart was playing the tune itself it a perfect blend of a heartbeat and piano. He sinks deeper and deeper into the music. Moving from one ear to the other, from one corner of his mind to the next leaving nothing in its wake.

The sound of music is all he hears. Not even the laughter and play of the dozens of kids on the bus can interrupt the peace within him. But just as he is fully enveloped in this feeling, he's awakened by the bus driver alerting him that they have reached the school.

"Hey kid, kid. Time to get off the bus let's go." He says. Navarro looks up at the bus driver. He can't believe they have made it to the school already. Many moments have past, as he cannot recount the ride to the school as he has been entranced by the sound of the piano and rapture it has created for his imagination.

He looks out of the bus window before wiping the sweat from his forehead. The bus driver looks at him and notices him sweating as if he were sick with a cold. He asks with a hint of concern. "Are you okay?"

Navarro doesn't say a word he just grabs his things and heads toward the exit. He races down the steps of the bus heading to the front entrance of the school. The bus driver just stares at him for a moment wondering to him-self what is wrong with this kid.

With nothing much to say he closes the doors to the bus and sits back in the driver's seat. Shaking his head with not much amazement he says.

"Crazy ass kids."

7

Something Beautiful

THE SANDS SEEP THROUGH THE HOURGLASS as the day wears on. Navarro's classroom is a buzz with the daily proceedings of learning or not so much as the teacher would suggest. The students try to stay attentive to the teacher as she goes over the lesson for the day. All but Navarro pay attention as the teacher delivers a lecture on social studies, a subject far less important than what is on his mind.

He sits staring at the clock waiting for it to strike twelve. Counting down the minutes, the seconds before he is able to leave and venture off to the music room where his mind has been fixed all morning. He has been thinking of nothing but that sound he heard the day before, that piano. Finally, the noon hour has come;

the bell rings and all the students file out into the hallway to line up for the walk to the cafeteria for lunch.

The small hallway is cluttered with children all trying to find their place in line to journey off down the hall for lunch. The sounds of hundreds of children pound against the walls. The teachers struggle to gain control of their classes as the kids, being stuck in their seats all morning find that this is a great opportunity to release all that energy that has been building inside of them.

"Come on class line up hurry up." One of the teachers directs to her students.

The students gather themselves and form some sort of order as they begin walking down the hallway. Melanie finds Navarro and walks over to him grabbing him by his hand trying to get his attention.

"Hi Navarro." She says with a huge bright smile on her face.

He returns her smile with one of his own. "Hi Melanie."

"Do you want to sit together today?" She asks.

He quickly responds. "Okay." He doesn't want to miss an opportunity to sit with his new friend, perhaps to him his only friend.

Melanie notices that Navarro isn't holding any lunch so she inquires as to what he will be eating. "So, what did you bring for lunch today?" She asks.

Navarro looks lost for a second before answering. "I didn't bring anything."

"Its okay you can have some of mine if you want." She replies.

He agrees to join in on her lunch as they continue to walk down the hall leading to the cafeteria. While walking to lunch they pass the music room. Something sparks a light in Navarro as he remembers this was his original mission during lunch. He stops for a moment and peeks into the room.

Melanie growing curious asks, "What are you doing."

"Hey, you go ahead I will meet you later." He tells her in order to give him some time to explore what awaits him in the music room. Melanie being the inquisitive person that she is asks more questions. "Why, what are you going to do?"

He quickly responds. "Nothing, I will meet you later okay." Melanie is worried because she sees the curiosity in Navarro's eyes, and she doesn't want him to do anything to get himself in trouble. Regrettably she complies and makes her way to the lunchroom. Before walking away, she makes sure she tells him to "hurry up".

"Okay I will." He replies, but now its time to venture further to find the source of the music he heard. Navarro looks around for a second and then sneaks into the music room hoping no one saw him enter. Unbeknownst to him, the object of his desire a beautiful black piano sits in the corner of a very large room.

He slowly walks into the room finding himself now in the center. He stands in the center of the room admiring the collection of famous faces on the walls. None of which are familiar to him.

The black and white photos are a mystery, but he realizes that these people must be important figures in music to have their faces on the wall.

He stands in silence surveying the room. He notices the piano sitting in the corner and becomes intrigued. He walks over to it slowly. Upon reaching it he touches it ever so gently. He begins to rub the side of it, stroking it like he is brushing the beautiful mane of a black stallion.

He has never witnessed something so beautiful. He makes his way around the piano. Touching the side, sliding his little fingers up and down against the body of the piano frame. He moves from one end to the other slowly to the front of the piano finding a bench resting there.

He pulls out the bench and gingerly touches one of the keys of the piano. The sound startles him at first unaware that even the slightest touch would make such a loud sound. He looks around to see if the sound alerted anyone, he doesn't want to be caught playing around on the piano. If caught he is sure that he would be sent to the principal's office and the thought of getting in trouble at school would surely cause trouble for him at home.

He quickly looks around before gathering himself to play another note. Slowly one note turns into two, and two into three. The notes though beautiful make no sense to him. He thinks back for a moment to what he heard the other day as he passed by the music room. That sound was the most beautiful sound his ears ever came to know.

He closes his eyes as notes begin to play in his head. Subtle at first, slowly finding their way from his mind to his ears then his chest as his heart begins to pound with every note he remembers. He opens his eyes and places his hands down on the piano as if he had been taught to do so correctly. He draws back to the first note he remembers and simultaneously the note rings in his head as his fingers make the sound a reality.

He plays the notes for a while just a mixture of sound and unorthodox melody. Suddenly something clicks in his head and his fingers and the notes begin to blend one after the other.

Note after note the song comes together. The more and more he plays the more complete it becomes. So much so it is as if he studied the song for days. His hands become a craftsman's hands. Building a beautiful piece of art, like a stonecutter carving away at a piece of marble to reveal an astonishing statue underneath.

He plays more soundly, vigorously touching the keys as they give way to his every notion. His heart becomes the tempo for which he gauges his play. Emotion gives way to sound, sound gives way to song and the feeling he had been so craving warmth, love, affection, and bliss he's found right beneath his fingers in the melodies and sounds of the piano.

Navarro continues to play becoming stronger and more fluid in his movements. His eyes are tightly shut as he plays letting his body and mind escape him. Letting go of control and restraint his heart drives his performance. He plays what he feels and what feels natural. Moving his hands from one end to the other stronger and faster he plays. Lost within the sound of music again he has found an escape from reality.

As Navarro plays, he is unaware that he is not alone. The music teacher has actually been in his office asleep. Trying to rest before his next class Mr. Browning, a very slim gray-haired older man sits in his reclining chair with his feet propped on his desk.

While napping he is slowly awakened by the sound of what appears to be his piano. Taking a minute to wake himself he realizes that yes, it is coming from the music room. But he wonders, "*Who could it be*" playing so beautifully yet none conformed. He jumps from his seat opens the door and walks out to investigate. Never has he heard such a sound by someone other than himself at the school. Furthermore, to his knowledge he is the only one capable of playing the piano at the school. The curiosity is mounting within him.

Navarro sits at the piano continuing to play. His eyes tightly closed as he loses himself within the music and melody of the piano. The sound of Mozart's *Piano Concerto* fills the air. Slowly Mr. Browning makes his way into the room. He first notices the room is empty. He looks over at the piano and doesn't see anyone sitting there. He knows there is someone there, so he makes his way around the room to the back of the piano. He is amazed at what he finds. Behind the keys sits a little boy playing Mozart like he has done it all his life. Mr. Browning stands in amazement, making sure he doesn't interrupt.

As Navarro plays, he begins to reach the end of his mini concert. Drawing to a close as the last note drops, he hears someone clapping behind him. Startled he turns around shocked to find the teacher standing there. Navarro finds himself embarrassed and afraid. He doesn't know what will come next. He knows he shouldn't have been there, but he couldn't help himself. After a moment of fear his feelings shift to being puzzled. He is amazed at Mr. Browning's reaction. Something he did not expect, Mr. Browning is actually amazed that Navarro was the one he found playing the piano.

Enthused he says to Navarro, "Wow that was great! How did you learn to play that?" Navarro for a moment is afraid to answer. He's not sure if Mr. Browning's reaction is genuine or a setup. Navarro sits speechless, for sure that he was about to find himself in the principal's office for sneaking in the music room. He doesn't know what to say. Mr. Browning inquires further. "Who taught you how to play that? How long have you been playing"?
Navarro shrugs his shoulders to relay, "I don't know."

"Well that was amazing." Mr. Browning becomes increasingly interested.

"Who teaches you?" He asks.
Navarro searching for an answer responds in a soft voice. "Nobody."

Mr. Browning can't believe what he just heard. "You mean to tell me that you don't have a teacher?" He asks. Navarro lowers his head and responds.

"No, I just heard you play it yesterday."
Amazed yet again by what Navarro is saying to him Mr. Browning's mind begins to race. Trying to take hold of the fact that this kid with no training has just played something so beautiful he can't believe it wasn't taught to him or at least practiced by him on a frequent basis.

Mr. Browning thinks for a moment then tries to sit down next to Navarro. The sudden move startles Navarro as he leaps from the bench to create distance between himself and Mr. Browning.

Mr. Browning also startled pauses for a moment. He holds out his hand and inquires. "What's wrong?" Navarro stands back a few feet as to not get to close to him.

"It's okay I won't hurt you." Mr. Browning conveys in a nurturing tone waving his hand to bring Navarro in closer.

"I want to play something for you. See if you can play it. It goes like this."
Mr. Browning collects himself and places his fingers on the piano. At that moment a visitor interrupts them. Melanie growing concerned has come to seek out Navarro.
As she rushes into the room all attention is placed on her. Mr. Browning turns from the piano to face her, removing his hands from the keys.

"Well hello Melanie, come on in. I was just sitting here with a new friend." He says.

Not missing a beat, she speaks "Hi Mr. Browning." She replies. All the while reaching out to grab Navarro by the arm. "Sorry Mr. Browning, but me and Navarro have to go to lunch before it's over."

Turning to Navarro Mr. Browning addresses him. "Oh, so your name is Navarro" He reaches his hand out to shake Navarro's hand. "Well its nice to meet you, young sir."

Before Navarro can answer, Melanie scoops him up. In a rush she drags Navarro from the room. "Okay Mr. Browning, we gotta go see you later bye." The two of them hand in hand rush out of the room. S quick as she arrived, the both of them are gone out of sight. In the hallway outside the music room Melanie stops for a moment.

"What were you doing?" She questions. "You could've gotten in trouble."
Navarro responds softly. "I just wanted to play."

Her concern is well noted. She senses that Navarro understands so she doesn't want to upset him any further

"It's okay. Come on let's go eat before lunch is over. I saved you some of mine"
She says.

The two of them rush off to the cafeteria. Back in the music room Mr. Browning still sits amazed at what he just heard. His mind still not wanting to believe that it came from this young 10-year-old boy.

Before shutting the key cover, he taps a few of the piano keys just to make sure for himself that the piano is not possessed or rigged by some mysterious unseen force. He then gets up and makes his way back to his office again astonished and amazed. Before closing the door to his office, he turns the light off then on again to look once more at the piano.

He shakes his head in an attempt to erase thoughts of what jut happened. He just can't believe what he has heard, even more so who was actually playing it. His mind soon gives way to reality and he suggests, it must be impossible for this kid to play without formal teaching. Of course, the thought of a modern day protégé is too much to bear so the thought of "it must be training" is easier to swallow allowing him to regress back to his corner to finish his nap. "Yes, that must be it," he says to himself. Mozart has not been reincarnated in this little child. "He must've been trained".

8

After School

THE SCHOOL DAY IS OVER, and all the kids are rushing to their buses for the ride home. Those that are not riding buses are waiting on their parents. As the last bus leaves and the crowd of kids begins to clear. Navarro sits on the steps of the school holding his book bag while he talks to Melanie and waits for his ride to arrive.

"Who's picking you up today?" Melanie asks with that inquisitive high-pitched voice. Navarro replies, "My mom." Melanie jumps at the chance to get Navarro to open up a little more. She begins to ask him a series of questions.

"My dad is coming to pick me up. What's your dads name?" She asks.

The question strikes a chord in Navarro as he just stares at Melanie for a moment. Almost as if he is registering what answer to give her. After a moment he replies.

"I don't know I never met him before."

"You've never met him before?" She asks, as only a little kid can. The response to her question seems a little unbelievable to her.

Navarro dips his head. "No, I haven't." he says softly. "My mom doesn't talk about him much."

Melanie, sensing that something is wrong with him switches the direction of the conversation over to herself. She offers, "Well my mom and dad aren't together anymore. They say that they have to figure some things out. My sister says they are getting a divorce."

Navarro lifts his head. "Divorce? What's that?"

Melanie, becoming a little sad, lowers her head. "I don't know exactly."

"Will they still be your mom and dad?" Navarro asks curiously.

"Yeah." she pauses for a moment. "Well I think so. It's kind of like they are your parents, but they don't live together anymore. You visit one of them on the weekends and you stay with the other. Or at least that's what my sister says."

Navarro takes in what Melanie is saying. He sees this as an answer to his problems at home. Excitement grows within him for a moment. Soon after he comes back to reality as his excitement turns to despair. He figures his mom would never leave the situation they are in. Since she will not leave, he has no way out.

His head drops in disappointment. "My mom would never leave Wayne."

Just as he says this Melanie's dad pulls up and blows the horn for her to come over to the car. "Well that's my dad, I have to go. I will see you tomorrow though. Okay?"

"Okay." Navarro says waving goodbye to her slowly. Before reaching her dad's car, Melanie turns back and runs toward Navarro. As soon as she makes it to him, she leans down to him and grabs him around the neck hugging him tightly.

She finds only a few words to say. "Its okay Navarro. Things will be okay." This is all she offers, but it is enough to comfort him. He hugs her back tightly only for a brief second before she let's him go and runs off to meet her dad. Before jumping in the back seat, she turns and waves at Navarro again. He waves goodbye and watches as she climbs into the car. Melanie's small frame disappears behind the huge car door as it closes the only thing showing is the tip of her hair. Before the car pulls away, she lifts herself up against the window to wave goodbye once again before the car quickly pulls out of sight.

Time passes as the last of the students find their rides. At this point everyone has left but Navarro. All the buses have left, and all the children have gone, while Navarro sits alone on the school steps. A few of the faculty members notice Navarro sitting out on the steps as they leave for home. One by one they drive off thinking to themselves why this little boy hasn't been picked up yet, but none stop to ask or offer any assistance to him. All they can do is look at him as he looks back at them, neither saying a word to one another.

An hour goes by and Navarro still sits waiting on his mother to arrive. He doesn't move because he knows that any minute, she could pull up to get him and of course he doesn't want to disappoint his mother by not staying put until she arrives.

After sitting a little longer, the last of the faculty members leave. Out of the side door exit's the music teacher Mr. Browning. He notices Navarro sitting there so he goes over to talk to him.

"Navarro, right?" he says. Setting his briefcase down on the steps.

"What are you still doing here, are you waiting for someone?"

Navarro shyly responds. "My mom comes to pick me up after school."

Mr. Browning inquires a little more. "Your mom huh? Okay so what time is she coming? Did she tell you exactly?"

Shaking his head Navarro slowly responds. "No, she didn't."

Mr. Browning pauses for a moment to assess the situation. He doesn't want to let Navarro know what he is thinking, but the look of concern is written on his face. How could a mother leave her child sitting here all evening?

He moves closer to Navarro. "Well do you mind if I sit here and wait with you?" Navarro moves over a little so that Mr. Browning can sit down.

The two of them sit quiet for a few seconds until Mr. Browning recalls the events earlier in the music room. "Navarro today you played that piano like I've never seen someone your age play before. It was great." Navarro reserved doesn't respond. Mr. Browning tries again to connect with him.

"And you say you have never had lessons before. That's amazing. Where did you get such skill? Man, if I had half your talent when I was your age, I guess I would be a much better teacher today." He releases a slight laugh as he nudges Navarro on his knee.

Navarro still remains unresponsive. Mr. Browning then tries to shift the conversation to something he thinks will get Navarro to open up to him.

"So where does your mom work? What does she do?" He asks.

Navarro begins to show some signs of interest. "She's a nurse. She works at the hospital." he says.

Mr. Browning seeing the opening continues. "Does she always pick you up from school?" Navarro replies back. "Most times she does. Sometimes I ride the bus."

"Are you sure she didn't want you to ride the bus today?" Mr. Browning asks.

Navarro looks at him with a look of concern and a bit of irritation at the question. He is sure of what his mother said to him and he never wants to go against her word.

"She said she was coming to get me." He says with a more defiant tone.

Mr. Browning pauses for a moment to back away from upsetting Navarro.

"Hmm I understand, but maybe she forgot this time." Navarro immediately responds. "She never forgets."

Mr. Browning thinks to himself for a moment before coming up with a solution to the problem that will benefit the two of them. "Well since you have been sitting out here for some time now, I think I should take you home." he says to Navarro.

Though it does in fact solve the problem Navarro doesn't seem too enthused by the suggestion. "I can't my mom said to wait. She will come she always comes. If she comes and I'm not here she will be mad at me."

Mr. Browning tries to explain the current situation in a manner to which he feels Navarro would be receptive to.

"I see, but it's getting late and I'm sure your mom wouldn't want you sitting here in this cold all evening. You just may get sick. Besides it will start to get dark soon."

Navarro doesn't respond he just looks down at the book bag he's holding in his hands. Mr. Browning attempts to rational the situation again.

"I tell you what, I will make a deal with you." This sparks Navarro's interest. He turns to Mr. Browning and listens. "You let me take you home today, and you can come by the music room tomorrow and play the piano all you want."

This idea sounds very inviting to Navarro. He thinks for a moment, rolling the idea around in his head.

"Okay, but what if my mom comes and I'm not here?" He asks.

Mr. Browning quickly comes up with a solution "Okay I tell you what we will do. We will leave word with the front desk that I have taken you home just in case your mom shows up soon. Does that sound okay?"

Navarro agrees as they both quickly rise from the cold steps and gather their things. They walk up the steps making their way to the front doors. Mr. Browning opens the door allowing Navarro to enter first.

They walk in together shaking off the cold as they head to the principal's office. As the huge steel doors close crashing together as if the school itself swallowed them whole they disappear behind them.

9

A Fading Light

AS THE LIGHT OF DAY FADES and the leaves of autumn rush across the front lawn of Navarro's house all is quiet. Mr. Browning pulls up in front of the house as they notice no one is home. Mr. Browning pulls the car to the curb and stops. Navarro peers out of the window to see if anyone is home. He doesn't see his mother's car and deep down he prays that Wayne isn't inside. Mr. Browning turns the car off and leans over to look out the window. "Is your mom home?' He asks.

Navarro doesn't say a word he just shrugs his shoulders an indication that he doesn't know. Mr. Browning motions for him to get out of the car so they can walk to the front door.

"Hmm, well let's see if someone is home." he says opening his door and taking a step outside of the car.

Navarro gets out of the car and runs to the front door quickly up the steps one foot after the other. He reaches the front door and finds that it is already unlocked.

He pushes the door open and disappears inside. Mr. Browning curious as to what is going on slowly makes his way to the house navigating each step as he walks after Navarro with the intentions of having a conversation with whomever is at home.

Ahead of him Navarro walks through the door to find his house in a chaotic state, like a tornado ran through his home. He stands in the doorway looking around the room. He sees broken glass and furniture turned on its side, certain he already knows what has taken place, as this scene is all too familiar to him.

He glances to his left and right registering in his mind all that has happened in his home. Surveying the area, they see pieces of glass littering the floor. The light of the setting sun shining through the windows makes the glass shimmer as if it were hundreds of diamonds.

Broken pictures of him and his mother lay across the floor as shattered glass from the coffee table litter the floor beneath his feet and all around him. Finally, his eyes rest and focus on something in the far corner of the living room. He stands with a stoic look on his face as he focuses more. After a moment of calm, he realizes what he is seeing. The body of his mother lay dormant on the floor, the back of her head looks as if it had been bathed in blood.

He walks slowly over to her with a facial expression devoid of any feeling. Step by step he comes within reach of her. His little feet and the weight of his body crush the glass that marks the path toward his mother. He reaches her and kneels down in front of her and places his hand on her forehead. He strokes her head for a moment and without crying out or saying a word his eyes begin to water. At that moment Mr. Browning enters the room. He surveys the damage and takes note of all the things out of place. He doesn't see Navarro at first, so he calls out to him.

"Navarro, are you okay?" He turns to his right and sees Navarro in the corner.

"Oh my God." He says with a look of shock and amazement on his face.

He watches as Navarro sits there on the floor stroking his mother's head. Frantic Mr. Browning rushes over to him. "Navarro, oh my God. Son step away, we will get help."

Mr. Browning rushes out of the room in search of a phone to call for help.

Navarro knowing that it is too late lays his head on his mother and wraps his arms across her body as if he is protecting her from anything else that may come. He then begins to break down and release all the cries and frustrations that are built within him as he weeps and cradles his mothers' body. Mr. Browning makes his way back into the room and rushes over to Navarro kneeling down on the floor next to him.

"Navarro its okay, it's going to be okay." He says as his voice cracks with every word. He can't believe what he is witnessing.

He tries to pull Navarro away from his mother but to no avail. Navarro clutches his mother tightly. He wraps his arms around her as if he is trying to prevent her from leaving him behind. He knows what this means, she has left him for good. He can't let go of her. He won't let go of her.

After trying a second time Mr. Browning leaves him alone and sits next to him placing his face in his hands attempting to wipe away the tears of sorrow, he sheds for this little boy who has just lost his mother violently. All feelings of hope have left his body, as he knows that Navarro's mother is dead.

He knows there is nothing he can do so he sits and waits. Not only does he feel saddened that there's nothing he can do to help, but that Navarro has had to witness the death of his mother at the hands of such a horrific act. Silently he wonders and prays to himself wishing that Navarro will somehow make it through this, but he knows that only time and God will reveal that answer.

10

Broken Pieces

ALTHOUGH THE SUN IS SHINING, there are no rays of sun shining down on Navarro as he and his family bury his mother Karen. As the reverend says the last words over the gravesite, Navarro sits in his seat and stares at the coffin. The reverend, bringing his sermon to a close takes note of how Karen leaves behind her son and a beloved family. There are no dry eyes all are showing their emotion with little to no control as it is a sad affair, a motherless child.

As the final words are spoken the family disperses. Navarro, clutching a white rose stands in front of the casket alone trying to gather the last bit of his mother's essence before he has to say goodbye to her forever.

The family comprised of Navarro's aunt and uncles stand off to the side and discuss where Navarro will go now that his mother has passed and is no longer here to take care of him. As the family gathers their discussion turns to a bout of excuses and or complaints. The first to speak is Navarro's aunt.

"Well I can't take him. I have three already, and I'm struggling as it is." she says.

His uncle speaks next. "I wish there was something I could do but I lost work and me and my wife are having a hard time right now."

Navarro stands at his mothers' coffin devoid of the noise going on behind him. He watches as the grave attendant's readies the coffin to be lowered into the six-foot depth it hovers above.

Through all the chaos and arguing between his family one voice of reason is heard, which puts and end to the argument. Navarro's grandfather Delray speaks "I will take him." Everyone stops and looks at him.

Delray, also known as "Papa D" is a slender built gray-haired man who wears the struggles he has been through in life on his face. He 50 years have taken a toll, but they have also shaped his existence. He stands before the family and in a majestic and defiant tone he says again "I will take him".

The family stands in silence not believing what they just heard.

Navarro's aunt tries to reason with him. "Papa you're getting to old to raise a child. We will figure something out." she says to him.

Again, a defiant Delray speaks out. "I said I would take him. The boy needs love and caring. Not sympathy from those of you who don't know what to give him or what to do with him."

They try once again to interject. Delray raises his hand to indicate the conversation is over he has spoken. Delray has given his final word and the family goes silent. He turns his back and walks toward Navarro. Navarro just stands and watches as the grave attendants lower his mother into the ground.

As Delray walks up behind Navarro, he stops for a moment to give Navarro one last second to be with his mother. Once the coffin reaches its final resting place Delray comes up behind Navarro and places his hand on his shoulder to comfort him.

His voice raspy yet strong delivers his words with eloquence.

"Come on son, let's go home."

Before walking away Navarro throws the white rose into the grave pit and watches as it crashes against the shiny coffin. Without a word he stands there waiting. Waiting for a sign or just waiting for his heart and mind to accept his goodbye.

This of course is his way of saying goodbye to his mother. He turns as Delray reaches out his hand to Navarro. He grabs Navarro by the hand and the two begin to make the long walk out of the cemetery to Delray's car.

As they reach the car Delray opens the door for Navarro and ushers him into the passenger's seat. He helps him adjust the seat and make sure that he fastens his seat beat around his waist.

Before shutting the car door, he asks if Navarro is okay making sure the seatbelt isn't too tight around him. After closing the door, he walks to his side and before starting the car he looks over at Navarro. Noticing that this ordeal is still taking a toll on him he tries to give Navarro a sense of belonging.

"It's going to be okay son. I'm here now, it's time to go home."

Delray pulls off leading Navarro to his new home. During the drive the noise of the city is drowned out by the sound of jazz playing on the radio. Old school jazz of Miles Davis serve as a soundtrack for the sprawling buildings Navarro witnesses as he stares out of the car window in amazement.

One by one the buildings seem to get bigger and bigger. He keeps peering out the window trying to assess his new surroundings, such a change from the suburban life he had grown to know. The landscape changes from buildings to an elevated train something Navarro has seen before. This is surely going to be an experience for him. They finally reach their destination, Delray's Downtown Chicago apartment.

As they pull up and stop Navarro gets out of the car and takes a look at his new home. It's an older classic looking home, seeming to have been built many years ago. He looks up at the 6-story building that is now his new home, devoid of Wayne but lacking his mother. Navarro stands in front of the home as his grandfather gathers his bags from the car.

He surveys the area for a moment looking at the home and surrounding area thinking to himself "how am I going to make it without my mom".

"Come on son, I've got your bags. Let's go inside." Delray directs as he places one hand on Navarro's shoulder leading him down the sidewalk to the front door.

As he reaches the door, he pauses waiting for his grandfather to unlock and open it. The door opens Delray walks in, a hesitant Navarro follows. Closing the door behind him Navarro stands with his back to the door as his eyes gaze across the living room.

First, he notices the many musical instruments laying around on the floor and hanging from the walls. He lets his eyes wander around taking in all that surrounds him. He notices the number of pictures on the wall, black and white photos of famous jazz faces. From Miles Davis to Billie Holiday some of the same faces that draped the walls of the music room at his school. He walks over to them as his grandfather exits the room. Making his way from one room to the next Delray walks to the bedroom to put Navarro's bags away.

As he walks out of sight toward the back, he talks to Navarro about the arrangements he has made. "I have set you up in the back bedroom. I've got everything taken care of for you so don't worry about anything."

Navarro walks over to the pictures on the wall and stares at them analyzing every frame. Delray walks back into the living room and notices Navarro investigating the photos. Noticing one photo that Navarro is surveying he says to him. "That one is of Ray Charles. The one next to him is Sam Cooke", he says.

Navarro looks at the photo with an unfamiliar look and asks. "Who?" Delray stunned responds quickly. "What!? Son Sam Cooke was one of the greatest soul singers to ever pick up a microphone." Navarro looks at the photo again as if to say, *"what's soul"*?

He then turns to his grandfather and asks him to tell more about the photos.
Obliged Delray finds a nearby stool and moves closer to Navarro. Taking a seat next to him he begins to run down the names of the characters in the other photos.

"That's Louis Armstrong there. And that man there was John Coltrane. The guys behind him were his band. All of them were great musicians back in their day. Do you know what jazz son is?"

Navarro slowly shakes his head to imply an affirmed no. Delray's eyes light up, as he can't believe Navarro has not been introduced to such an influential genre of music.

"I've got some records I will play for you. A young man such as yourself shouldn't be deprived of all the greats. Wait right here I will be back" he says.

Delray gets up and walks to the back room of the house. Navarro lets his eyes wander again. He glances across the room and through the glass doors of the study he sees a piano sitting in the corner. His eyes grow wider as he gets up and walks into the study.

Not as classy and sleek as the piano at his school but it intrigues him just the same. As he walks around the piano, he can still hear his grandfather speaking to him from the back of the house. "I've got a few Charlie Parker and Nat Cole records too." He yells out to him.

Navarro sits down at the piano and stretches his fingers across the old keys, some broken and some out of tune as he begins to play. His grandfather suddenly stops speaking, as he hears the sound of music coming from the study. A somber sound begins to resonate throughout the house.

The sound can be categorized as a reflection of someone's pain. It is a song never before heard by Delray. Very much out of tune, yet still beautiful. He walks slowly to the study and sitting at the piano he sees Navarro playing with tears in his eyes. Delray walks over to him and places his hands on his shoulders. Navarro immediately stops playing and wraps his arms around his grandfather. Delray holds him tightly as they embrace. Navarro again letting out all the frustration and anger built inside of him squeezes his grandfather and cries out to him.

"Why did she leave me papa, why?" Delray tries to calm him but allows him to release the hurt and pain locked within him. "Its okay son. Let it out." he says as he holds Navarro tightly against his chest.

Not able to hold back his emotion slowly tears begin to flow from Delray's eyes. Navarro's emotion shifts from pain to confusion. The loss of his mother has his feelings raging in all directions. "I don't know why she left me papa. I don't know why. I thought she loved me." Navarro says as his tears flow. His voice shaken and cracking with each word.

Delray tries again to make some sense out of what Navarro is feeling and all that has happened. "Shhh, it's going to be okay." He says gathering himself.

"You're here with papa now. It's okay. You can be angry if you want, but understand your mother loved you with everything she had. She's still with you son. In your heart, that's where you gotta keep her. Keep her there and never forget her." Navarro tries to shake his emotion while holding tight to his grandfather.

"It's hard papa, it's so hard." Delray pauses for a moment and lifts Navarro's head to wipe his eyes. He then says in a strong and enduring voice, "I know son, but you have to use that pain and that anger. Use it to make you stronger." Navarro looks back at him. Feeling neglected and defeated he says, "I don't know how papa. I don't know how."

Delray again wipes Navarro's tears and looks him square in the eye. "I heard you playing that piano. It took a lot of emotion and feeling to play like that. Use it to become better, stronger. Navarro you can do anything you want in life and I promise you that your mother will be there in the end when it's done. You just have to believe. Believe in yourself and you can make it through this. We will make it through this together"

Navarro is drawn into what his grandfather is saying to him. "Will you teach me?" he asks.

Delray quickly answers back. "Yes. Yes, I will. Come on I will teach you."

Navarro clears his face and pays close attention as his grandfather positions himself in front of the piano and goes over the keys. Delray sounds out each note as he plays and at that moment the two of them take the first steps on a journey that will bring them forever closer together. Although an invited journey for both, unbeknownst to Navarro, his life is about to take on many different changes....

11

Life's Song

MONTHS HAVE PASSED AND, ON THIS DAY, THE EARLY MORNING brings a cool breeze across the waters of Lake Michigan. Delray and Navarro sit at the end of a pier fishing. Bundled in a jacket and cap both brave the cold not so much to catch fish but Delray sees this as an opportunity to bond with Navarro. "Have you ever been fishing before son?" Delray asks.

Navarro thinks to himself for a moment before answering. "No, me and my..." He pauses and places his head down before continuing. "My mom never had time to take me anywhere."

"Well that's okay." Delray explains. "It doesn't take much skill to catch fish. It's all about one fundamental thing that everyone should possess."

Navarro lifts his head and asks. "What's that?" Delray pauses for a moment then reveals the answer. "Patience."

Navarro of course confused looks out at the water. They both sit in silence for several minutes. Navarro is unnerved by the quiet. He looks out at the water and listens to it crash against the rocks on the shore. The sun shines, but of course the cold air coming of the lake makes this fishing trip one not so much about fun.

Suddenly a frustrated and fidgeting Navarro breaks the silence. "How long do we have to wait for the fish to bite?" he asks.

His grandfather quickly quiets him down. "Shhh you have to be quiet and patient. Just listen to the wind. If you're too loud the fish will hear you and run away."

Navarro doesn't understand. He's growing more impatient by the second. "Why does it take so long though?" he asks.

Delray again tries to quiet him. "Navarro you have to be very patient. The fish will come on their own time. I want you to do something for me."

Navarro seizes the opportunity to do something other than sitting and waiting. "Okay what do you want me to do?" he asks.

"I want you to close your eyes." Delray instructs. Navarro closes his eyes. Delray then asks him a series of questions.

"Okay, I want you to keep you eyes closed and tell me what you hear." Navarro responds. "I don't hear anything."

"Shhh, listen. Tell me what you hear." Delray instructs again.

Navarro goes very quiet as he tries to listen to whatever his grandfather is asking him. A few minutes pass and nothing. Navarro's eyes pop open. "I don't hear anything", he says again.

Delray once more directs him to close his eyes and listen. "This time I want you to listen not to what you think you should hear, but to what you are able to hear."

Navarro takes a deep breath and lets out a long sigh before doing what his grandfather has asked him to do. He closes his eyes and begins to listen. After a few moments he is ready to give up.

Keeping one eye closed he opens another peeking over to look at Delray.

Delray begins to speak to him again. Navarro closes his eyes quickly holding them tightly shut. He hears his grandfather next to him.

"Listen. Just listen. Tell me what you hear." Navarro goes very quiet trying to concentrate as hard as he can to hear any and all sounds that may be there. Becoming impatient he breathes in and releases a sigh heavy enough that his grandfather notices.

"Listen to the sounds around you. Tell me what you hear." Delray explains. "Listen to the sound between the wind. Listen to the whistle, very soft and subtle. Can you hear it?"

Navarro listens carefully then all of a sudden it becomes clear to him. Excited he says. "Yes, papa I can hear it. I can hear it now."

Delray quiets him again. "Shhh son, just listen." Navarro listens intently. Delray lays his pole down on the pier and places his hand on Navarro's chest.

"Tell me now, what do you hear?" he asks.

Navarro shifts from listening to the wind to the sound of his heart. "I hear my heart beating." Delray again asks. "What do you hear?"

Navarro listens again, "It sounds like a drum," he says. Delray shows a slight smile before saying. "Now, you are listening. The sounds around us are not just noise. Listen not just to the wind but the sound the wind makes. Listen not just to your heart, but also to the beat your heart creates. Everything around you creates sound. The blending of that sound makes a song. Each song is different and beautiful in its own way."

Navarro begins to smile. "I can hear it papa, I hear the song." He says with excitement. Delray removes his hand from Navarro's chest. "Good, open your eyes." he says.

Navarro opens his eyes and at that moment Delray points to his fishing pole. Navarro watches in amazement as his cork bobbles up and down in the water. "I've caught one, I've caught one!" he yells out to his grandfather.

"Pull him in." Delray says. Navarro pulls back hard on his pole as Delray grabs the fishing line to assist him. One huge yank and out of the water pops a huge fish. "Pull him in." Delray says.

Navarro responds. "I'm trying, help me."
Delray grabs onto the pole. They both pull on the pole and within an instant the fish is hoisted high in the air.

Flying through the air the fish flies from the water slamming down on the pier next to the two of them flopping around on its side. Excited they both embrace and take enjoyment in what Navarro has achieved. "Thank you, papa." Navarro says hugging his grandfather around his neck.

"You're welcome son. This was all your work. Do you know how you made this happen?" Delray asks. Navarro thinks for a moment searching for the answer. Suddenly it dawns on him. "Patience." he says with a huge smile on his face.

Delray looks at him and places his hand on his head. Not saying a word but confirming his answer with a smile and a kiss on his forehead.

They both look at the fish again and share a laugh together. Today this fishing trip has turned into a life lesson for Navarro. His grandfather looks down at him with pride, thinking to himself that Navarro has come so far since the passing of his mother but yet he has so much further to go.

Knowing this road will be long he is more than willing to endure all the twists and turns that this journey together will bring, all in an effort to provide Navarro with a sense of self and belonging. After a moment of taking pride in their catch the two of them cast their poles back into the water. Navarro learning from what his grandfather has just revealed to him sits still, patiently waiting for his cork to dip beneath the water. All the while he listens. He listens to the wind, to the birds, and to the sound of his heart beating. No longer beating in fear but for once with a beating that signifies accomplishment and happiness. This song, his song, is the song of Life.

12

The Protégé

THE SOUND OF MUSIC plays loudly throughout a nearly empty warehouse building. Delray and his band known as "PAPA D and THE CREW" rehearse for an upcoming show. Not only is Delray a fan of jazz, he is also a jazz trumpeter and vocalist the lead of his 7-piece band.

The band is comprised of Papa D, vocalist trumpeter. Donell drums, Quinton "Q" Prime, baritone sax, John Levingston, bass guitar and stand up bass, Kenneth "SMOOTH" Wilkes, tenor sax, Saucey 29 rhythm guitar and Pearl 35, piano. All middle-aged men and women living out their dreams and love for music in this band.

A very diverse mixture of ages and races yet all share a love and passion for music and the creation of music. Their love for music is mirrored by their love of performing.

While the band rehearses Navarro sits outside the huge loft space going over a scale of sheet music his grandfather gave him to study. He sits trying to focus on his study but the sound of music coming from the loft is commanding his attention.

As the band is rehearsing a few of the guys are becoming agitated because one of the members hasn't shown up yet. Pearl, the piano player has been consistently late for rehearsal and it's wearing on the guys in the band. Suddenly there's a break in rehearsal as one of the band members speaks out.

John, the bass player is the first to speak "Hey man this is getting to be a real headache. Papa D you need to do something about Pearl."

"Yea this is the fifth time she has been late for rehearsal," says Donell.

Now that these two have spoken up the rest of the guys find this as being a great opportunity to voice their opinions on the subject of Pearls lateness.

Quinton is next to chime in, "Right before a show date and she's late. What are we going to do if we can't find a piano player?" Just as he finishes the doors swing open and in rushes Pearl. The band goes quiet as all eyes watch as she throws all of her things on the floor and plops down on the piano stool.

Out of breath Pearl says, "Sorry I'm late guys I had a meeting."

Everyone looks around at one another for a moment then back at her. Pearl is a healthy woman standing 5 feet six weighing well over 190 pounds. Simultaneously the band turns to Papa D with looks to infer that he should do or say something about her tardiness. Before Delray can get a word out one of the members instigates a confrontation between Pearl and the band.

"A meeting huh? Are you sure about that?" says Kenneth. Usually he is the quiet one, but Pearls antics have grown tiresome to him as well.

Pearl looks at him stunned that he would even say such a thing to her. It's expected from the other members but not from him. She ignores him and continues to settle in at the piano. Suddenly John bursts out with his comments on her being late.

"Pearl Papa D has something he wants to talk to you about." Delray looks at him with a look of "*what have you gotten me into*" on his face.

Not missing a beat Donell adds, "Yea, he said he's tired of you being late." Again, Delray looks at both of them as if he can't believe they just threw him to the wolves like this.

Pearl becoming upset slams the cover over her piano keys and addresses both of them. "Papa aint said nothing to me so both of you need to shut the hell up" Delray quickly takes control of the conversation. Calmly he asks, "Pearl, why were you late?"

She responds. "I had a meeting."

Delray takes a moment to register what she has said before responding. "You know we have a show tomorrow."

Flustered Pearl tries to explain herself. "Well I had a meeting and I lost track of time. But I'm here now." Interrupting her Donell blurts out, "I'm sure it wasn't important. You should've been here."

Pearl becomes very aggravated by the attacks of the other guys. She instantly lashes out. "Shut up Donell, if I wanted your opinion, I would tell you to kiss my ass and tell me what it tastes like."

The band quickly draws back. Delray sensing that it has gone too far addresses Pearl again.

"Did this meeting have anything to do with that band uptown?" he asks.

Pearl's mouth drops as if she has been found guilty of a charge. Everyone goes quiet they had no idea of what she was doing. Through out all the noise Navarro has found it very hard to concentrate on his studies. He peeks inside the room from a crack in the front door.

Pearl scrambles to find an answer, "Papa D its nothing, I just went to check it out that's all." Delray explains, "Pearl when you joined The Crew, I told you that it was a commitment to us. That there couldn't be anything else."

Pearl tries to plead with him." Papa, I know, I know but…"

Delray swiftly interrupts. "I don't want to hear it. Pearl leave now." He points at the door demanding that she leave.

Pearl looks at him with a look of disbelief on her face. For a moment she freezes before picking her things up from the floor and swiftly exiting the room. She bursts through the front door and charges past Navarro. Through the doorway he looks back at the band and his grandfather with eyes wide open.

After a moment of congratulatory laughter at the move Delray has just made amongst the group, reality quickly begins to set in. They have realized that they now do not have a piano player for their upcoming engagement.

Donell, the most vocal member speaks up first. "Damn, we wanted you to do something about her being late not fire her. Now what are we going to do about a piano player? The show is tomorrow." he says.

Delray thinks to himself for a moment then surmises the answer. Something he had been pondering for a while now has come to fruition.

"Don't worry about that." he says reassuring the group that he has things handled. Delray walks to the door of the rehearsal hall. He opens the door and calls to Navarro. They both walk back into the room together with Delray's hand on Navarro's shoulder leading him over to the rehearsal area.

With a huge smile on his face Delray looks at the band then Navarro.

"Gentlemen meet your new piano player." he says motioning Navarro to the center of everyone. They look at one another for a moment then at Navarro before bursting out with laughter. Donell says first. "Man, it's a kid!"

Making a point that he's too young to join an adult group for a performance. The others echo his concerns. Delray looks down at Navarro then whispers in his ear. Navarro quickly rushes over to the piano and takes his place. Delray picks up his trumpet. He directs the guys to grab their instruments. "Try to keep up." he says to them as he winks at Navarro.

Delray begins to play a jazz riff on the trumpet and soon after Navarro joins in on piano. The two of them mesh together and start a jam session, slow in tempo then bursting to life with a swift movement.

Gradually the laughter in the room comes to an end as the grandfather and grandson combination is wowing the band members. One by one smiles appear on their faces and their apprehensions turns to confirmation in their minds that *"yes, this kid has got it"*.

Soon after they each pick up their instruments and begin to join in. As if they had been playing together for years they blend perfectly. They swing from jazz to rhythm and blues. The tempo shifts moving fast then slow then fast again showing a varying range that they all posses.

Once the session is complete applause echoes throughout the warehouse, they all concur that Navarro belongs in The Crew.

They each shake Navarro's hand and introduce themselves to him. Delray stands with his arms crossed nodding his head, thinking to himself "Navarro will finally have a place where he fits perfectly".

Navarro looks over at his grandfather and gives him the biggest smile he has ever smiled. His troubles over the past year have all seemed to disappear within a matter of minutes while playing with the band. His eyes become bright with desire for acceptance, and that acceptance has come in the form of a group of guys who will not only provide a support system for him, but a sense of appreciation for a craft that he possesses to which they all share. For in an instant his heart fully opens to accept what life may have in store for him.

13

Club Epiphany

THE COLD OF WINTER HAS RETURNED yet the nightlife of Downtown Chicago is ablaze. The atmosphere is electric outside Club Epiphany one of the hottest clubs in the downtown area. Though the club is known for the talent that graces its stage on many nights, this Friday night is a little different than most. Everyone has come to see Navarro the "Prodigy".

Navarro has grown from the shy reserved kid he used to be. He has grown into an accomplished composer, singer, and writer. Well learned in many different genres of music, and affluent in over a dozen instruments. The basic structure of music taught to him by his grandfather has carried Navarro and molded him into the young musical genius he has become today at the age of 24.

A crowd runs from block to block all coming to catch a glimpse of the hometown wunderkind.

Different sexes and races, all ages wait in line for the show. Posters litter the outside walls of the club reading:

"CLUB EPIPHANY PRESENTS~A NIGHT OF LOVE~PAPA D AND THE CREW FEATURING CHICAGO'S OWN PRODIGY NAVARRO LOVE"

Inside the sound of old school soul music plays loudly. On stage Papa D and The Crew are playing their rendition of Al Green's "I Can't Get next To You". Delray carries the lead while backed by his band. His aged soulful voice rips through the song as if he had written it himself.

Moving across the stage, his age now 64 doesn't show one bit as he performs as if he were in his 20's. As the last of those who came to the show try to find their seats, The Crew burns up the stage with their blend of jazz and soul, but one member is missing. Navarro hasn't joined the band for his portion of the set yet.

With all that's going on no one notices at first but now that his time draws near the band members begin to question one another while playing. Donell, the first to notice brings it to the others attention first.

"Psst, psst Smooth, Smooth. Where's Navarro?" he says speaking over the music as it plays. The others look around and try to peek backstage to find Navarro. Not able to find him they continue to play.

Delray, while singing notices the group growing concerned. He turns for a second and then notices Navarro isn't standing off stage and his set is almost near. He turns to Donell and questions with just motioning his eyes. Donell answers with a shrug of his shoulders signaling that he has no idea where Navarro may be.

They continue play as to not hinder the performance. Delray motions to one of the bouncers standing off stage to find Navarro before the song ends. The bouncer takes his queue and rushes backstage to search the dressing rooms.

With no regard for knocking he bursts through each door in hopes of finding Navarro before the next song begins. Back on stage, to ensure that they have enough time before the transition, Delray calls for the band to continue playing. Being the music lovers they are, The Crew doesn't mind. Who can resist an opportunity to perform and encore for a loving audience? Play continues as if nothing's wrong.

Things continue to heat up inside the club as a never-ending line of people continues to enter. While most enter from the front, the back door adjacent to the alley behind the club shows favor to those with connections. Also, beautiful women lucky enough to know the bouncers, occasionally enter here for free.

Tonight, we find three beautiful women attempting to enter. The group of ladies consists of Monica aged 24, a caramel skinned toned hazel-eyed woman with a slender medium build and shoulder length dark hair. Followed by Sherri 26, a more sophisticated woman. Smooth dark skin with natural full lips and toned body, she accentuates Afro centricity and class.

Last there is Paris 24, a beautiful fair skinned woman. She carries a slim dancer build with flowing black hair down her back. She is very shy in demeanor with dark eyes that seem to look straight through you gazing deep within your soul.

Monica, being the ringleader and typical club hopping man magnet, has brought her two friends out to see Navarro and the band play. She is a regular at the club and visits with the band on occasion.

"Come on girls we are going to be late." she says to her friends as they make their way to the backdoor entrance. The others are a little apprehensive about going out tonight, both for their own reasons.

Sherri races after Monica finding it very difficult to keep up wearing her 5-inch heels. "Slow down girl!" she yells to Monica. "I didn't even want to come out here tonight. You are lucky I need a drink right now."

Sherri catches Monica by the arm and stops her from leaving both her and Paris, who is lagging far behind. They both wait by the backdoor to give Paris a little more time to catch up. Paris finally meets up with the other two but the look on her face shows how she really feels about being out with them this night.

"You know I'm not sure about this." She confesses to Monica and Sherri.

They both look at her as if she has said something very wrong.

Monica tries to plead with her. "What do you mean you don't know? Girl it is freezing out here, let's go inside." Paris holds her head down as if something is weighing on her mind. "Boo what's wrong?" Sherri asks.

"Nothing I'm just tired." Paris replies. After a brief silence Paris attempts to explain her feelings. "It's just that…." She pauses for moment. Monica being the abrupt person that she is interrupts her. "I know you're not still worried about your recital, are you?"

Paris shyly looks down at her shoes. Sherri grabs Paris by the hand in an attempt to get her to open up. "What's wrong sweetie," she asks. Monica interrupts again. "She's worried about her recital."

Sherri ignores Monica and focuses on Paris. She places her finger on her chin and lifts her head. She asks again. "Sweetie what's wrong?"

Paris pauses for a moment. "Well it's just that I have this recital." Monica blurts out again. "I told you." Paris looks at her and rolls her eyes.

"This is very important to me. It could be my big break and I don't want to mess this up." Sherri tries to lift her spirits by pointing out her skills as a dancer. "Sweetie you have been practicing for a while now. You've got it." she says.

Monica places her hand on Paris' back in an attempt to show her support. "Look, it's not for another week, right? Come on you will be okay."

Paris' apprehensions begin to peel away slowly but still she has reservation about being out with her girls. Sherri and Monica continue in their attempts to convince Paris that its okay to just let go for a few hours and join them on their night out.

After a few more moments she gives in. Paris throws her feelings to the side and agrees to go inside. "Okay, okay I hear both of you." she says. "But if I don't make it through my dance recital the both of you are dead."

The girls laugh and brandish huge smiles, as they are happy that Paris has finally agreed to come inside. The girl's head for the backdoor and as they knock the door opens to reveal a huge muscular bald man behind it. He looks at the girls with a sly smirk on his face before giving them passage. "Follow me ladies." he says as he guides them down the dark hallway leading them to the club floor.

As the walkway opens up, they notice posters littering the walls, some of which highlights the main event of the night and Navarro as the headliner. They stop for a moment to comment, "He is nice." Monica says pointing at the poster. The other girls look up to fix their eyes on the colorful and huge poster. Sherri whispers to Paris,

"You know I usually don't agree with her, but she is right. He is fine." Paris tries to brush off what Sherri is saying as if she is not interested. As the ladies walk further down the hallway the music from the club floor grows louder. They hear it thumping against the walls.

They finally reach the main floor the lights illuminating the club and stage are quite a spectacle. Not the typical stage design or club this looks more like a concert performance. The ladies take it all in before finding their seats down front center stage.

Meanwhile backstage the search for Navarro continues. The club lights and music die out as the bouncer continues his search. He rushes down the winding hallway opening every door that he comes to making his way to the rear dressing rooms. Finally, he reaches Navarro's dressing room. Before bursting through the door, he knocks. He knocks once more then again and doesn't hear a sound.

He turns the doorknob and slowly opens the door. He finds Navarro sitting at his desk, his eyes fixed on a piece of paper in front of him.

"Navarro, Navarro." the bouncer calls out to him. Navarro sits still as if he is in a daze, he doesn't hear anything. The bouncer tries once more. "Navarro!" He yells out to him.

Navarro doesn't turn to acknowledge him, but he does respond.

"Yea." he says, still fixated on the sheet music in front of him.

"Papa D needs you on stage." The bouncer tells him. Still he doesn't make eye contact he just responds. "Be there in a minute."

Not missing a beat, he continues to look over the sheet music, making marks on it and erasing mistakes along the way while writing. Before leaving the room the bouncer just stares at him and shakes his head. He slowly closes the door and makes his way back to the stage floor.

On stage Papa D and The Crew begin to wrap up their session. The crowd is at the edge of their seats awaiting the next performance. The girls, led by Monica, get settled into their seats. "Okay here we go. We almost didn't make it." Monica says to the others.

Sherri looks around and surveys the club. "Girl this place is hot." she says to Monica, giving her stamp of approval on the atmosphere of the club.

Paris looks around and comments softly. "Yes, it is." Suddenly the lights in the club go very dim. Delray and his band have finished their set and the crowd begins to cheer. Through the noise of the crowd the club announcer can be heard.

Over the PA system in a low baritone voice he says. "That was Papa D and The Crew." The crowd again begins to applaud.

After a moment of applause, the crowd goes silent as anticipation grows for the main event. They all await Navarro to take the stage. Without warning the club announcer is heard over the club speakers. "Ladies and Gentlemen Club Epiphany is proud to bring you, Mr. Navarro Love."

The club erupts in applause as the music begins to play. The lights come up and a figure appears seated behind a piano. The illuminated colors of red, blue, and purple lights accent a stage surrounded by candles, creating a mood of romance and sure elegance.

Navarro begins to sing as the lights come up fully on his frame as he sits behind the piano. He plays a love ballad smooth and sensual. The words flow from his mouth to the ears of everyone in the club. Backed by The Crew he delivers a powerful performance. Delray stands off to the side of the stage and watches as Navarro performs.

Feeling proud and full of admiration he enjoys watching the shy young boy he raised blossom into a talented young man and performer. As Delray watches offstage a waitress comes up to him and nudges his shoulder. "He looks good tonight," she says. Delray looks at her then back at the stage displaying a bright smile he says, "Yes he does."

At their table the ladies sit in adoration of what they are witnessing. Along with every female in the club they hang on to Navarro's every word. All their eyes stay focused on him as he delivers the song in a strong and passionate way.

Monica makes a point to inform the girls once again of Navarro's appeal. "Oh my God he is so gorgeous" she says to them. Sherri nods her head in agreement. Paris stays focused on the stage performance. She sits very quiet staring at Navarro. She watches as he makes his way from behind the piano to center stage.

While performing he notices her. They make eye contact and at that moment he reaches a point in the song that he directs solely to her. He walks slowly to the edge of the stage the spotlight following his every move. He reaches the edge and points his finger directly at Paris. He sings to her,

"Can I be your eye's so that I may see what beauty sees. Would it be things I couldn't understand, Things I could not believe
Touch me love, mold me into the man God wants me to be.
For with you I am not afraid. For you are my destiny."

The two of them lock eyes, speaking to one another without saying a word letting the music whisper words that only they two can hear.

As the song draws to a close and the lights go dim. Paris continues to make eye contact. She stares as if she had been hypnotized during the performance. The lights come up and the crowd erupts with applause. The announcer comes across the house PA system. "Ladies and Gentlemen, Mr. Navarro Love." The crowds' applause grows louder pleased with the performance they have just seen.

Navarro and The Crew exit the stage as another band readies in the wing for their chance on stage. Monica suggests meeting the band after the show is over. "Hey after the set do you want to meet the band?" Sherri immediately responds, "Yes".

Paris continues to look off into space unaware of the question she was asked. Sherri nudges her elbow to grab her attention. "Hey girl did you hear?" Paris shakes off her daydream. "Huh, hear what?" she asks.

Monica leans over the table "We're going backstage after the show." Paris acknowledges by nodding her head. Softly she responds, "Yea, okay sure." The ladies go back to enjoying their drinks while awaiting the next performances on stage.

Paris settles back in her chair trying to shake off the effects of what she felt while Navarro was on stage. She looks down at her drink and gives way to a slight smile. Stirring her drink with her straw the thoughts swirl in her head unknowing that what she has just felt could be the beginning of something more. Beginning with a glance could there be something more there. She shakes it off and proceeds to focus on the stage.

As the lights go black the next band takes the stage. Paris shifts her attention from her drink to the performers. The band is a welcomed distraction. She is able to clear her head and focus on something other than Navarro and her upcoming dance recital at least for the moment. She relaxes a little in her chair. She looks out around the club takes a deep breath then exhales. She finally accepts the aspect of letting go and enjoying the moment with her friends.

After the shows end the club begins to close. Delray and The Crew make their way to the dressing room to relax and gather their equipment to leave. Navarro sits in his dressing room working on his composition for an upcoming concert. As he is working, he begins to feel a sharp painful headache. Nothing short of a migraine, but he tries to continue working. He shakes off the slow pounding thump in his head. At that moment his grandfather

Delray walks in the dressing room followed by The Crew. The Crew still excited about the performance comes in loudly congratulating one another.

Quinton the loudest member of the group screams out. "Man, that show was hot!" Jumping around the dressing room he cannot hold in his enthusiasm. As the rest of the band join in on the self-proclaimed pat on the back session, Delray looks over at Navarro and notices something is wrong with him. He walks over to him and places his hand on Navarro's shoulder.

"Is everything okay son?" he asks. Navarro's eyes stay fixed on the compilation in front of him. He slowly responds. "Nothing Papa."

Delray looks at him for a moment. He knows that there is more to the story, so he clears the dressing room. "Hey, you guys go ahead and grab everything so we can get out of here. I will catch up with you." he directs to the band.

They each grab cases full of instruments and head for the door. Kenneth, the last to leave informs Delray that "the guys are hungry and that they will wait outside."

Once the door closes Delray pulls his chair closer to Navarro. He gently places his hand on Navarro's and moves the pencil and paper from his hands. "What's wrong son?" he asks again.

Navarro leans back in his chair. "Nothing papa just a little headache that's all." he says, not convincing Delray.

"Okay, tell me what's really wrong." His grandfather insists.

"Are you concerned about the concert?" he asks. "Are you nervous about the show? You know its okay to be nervous."

Delray grabs Navarro's shoulder and shifts his body to face him. "Do you remember what I told you about being nervous?"

Navarro shows a little smile and nods his head. Delray looks him in the eye and instructs him to "let him hear it." Pushing Navarro to open up. "Come on, tell me."

Navarro takes a breath then recites what his grandfather taught him. "Nervousness is just displaced energy."

"Exactly!" Delray exclaims. "Use it son. Don't allow your nervousness to destroy your thinking. Use it to get better. Don't worry you will be fine."

Navarro relaxes in his chair as his grandfather pats him on the back while getting out of his chair. Navarro looks down at his composition and smiles. As Delray heads to the door he turns to Navarro.

"Besides if I were your age, I'd get up there with you, then you'd really have something to worry about."

Navarro looks back at his grandfather and with a look of reassurance he says to him. "You're not so old, old man."

Delray turns and walks to the door. Before leaving he says, "Yeah, the last 14 years haven't been as generous as you. I'm getting old son."

Navarro pauses for a moment as if to reflect on the many years that have passed. Delray walks out of the dressing room but before the door closes shut Navarro yells to him. "I love you pop!"

The door shuts but not before Delray yells back. "Love you too son."

Navarro takes a moment to gather his thoughts before looking back at his composition. He takes in a deep breath then exhales. He grabs his pencil and focuses his eyes back on his work. After a few moments he lifts his head and looks back at the door. His thoughts give way to the feeling of admiration that he has for his grandfather. He shakes his head in order to re-focus his thoughts to his work. He tries to re-insert himself into that deep place to which all his creative thoughts flow. He tries but fails.

Not able to regain his focus he grabs his composition, jumps from his chair, and rushes out of the dressing room door to catch up to his grandfather. Taking a break from writing he would rather spend the rest of his night having fun with his grandfather and the crew.

In the hallway he finds his grandfather. "So, you decided to join us." Delray says.
Navarro replies back. "Of course, I couldn't let you old guys have all the fun."

The two of them walk down the hallway leading to the back door together. "By the way, nice show." Delray says.

Navarro throws his arm around his grandfather's shoulder. "Thanks papa." He replies. Together they make their way to the exit. As they get closer to the back door the lights from the club fade and everything goes dim.

As the night grows longer many begin to leave the club and pour out into the streets. Behind the club, near the rear exit door, waits Monica, Sherry, and Paris. They stand in the cold waiting on The Crew to exit through the back door. Although they are eager to meet the band Sherry and Paris have grown tired of waiting as well as standing in the cold.

Monica a regular at the club and secretly aspiring part time singer has been trying to get the band to put her on stage for some time now. She views this as an opportunity to speak with Delray about joining the band. But the other girls are growing increasingly tired of waiting in the cold.

"How much longer is it going to be?" Asks Paris.

"Yes, it is getting late and very cold out here." adds Sherry.

The two of them stand there shivering rubbing their arms in a poor attempt to warm themselves. Monica tries to get the girls to hold out just a little while longer.

"Ladies look it shouldn't be too much longer." She pleads. "Besides, Paris don't even try it you know you want to meet Navarro."

Paris stops and rolls her eyes "Whatever!" Monica teases her more. "I saw how you were looking at him while he was on stage."

Sherry joins. "Yea I saw that too." Paris gives an embarrassing smile as her cheeks turn red. "I was not looking at him that way." she says. "Yea right." says Monica.

"It seemed like you wanted to just run up there on stage and give him some in front of everybody." The ladies share a laugh at Paris' expense. They continue to tease her all the while trying to keep their mind off the cold.

Suddenly the back door burst open and out pours The Crew followed by Delray then Navarro. They each greet the girls one by one as they file out of the club. Paris stands eager to see Navarro but tries to not let it show as she stands behind her two girlfriends.

Finally, they all come out. Paris sees Navarro and immediately she is drawn to him. Navarro doesn't notice her at first because he and his grandfather are speaking to one another.

"Hello fellas." says Monica.

Each one of the guys in the band simultaneously speaks back "Hello Monica." Monica looks around and notices Delray standing in the background. "Hello Papa D." she yells out.

Delray looks around to see who has just called his name. The Crew moves aside and creates a hole in the middle of the group as if they were the Red Sea being parted. Delray acknowledges Monica. "Hello Monica. How are you doing?" he says.

She responds back. "I'm fine. I'd be doing a lot better if you were to give me a solo one night." Delray cracks a smile, and simply says "No".

Monica stands there with her jaw dropped speechless. The Crew shift to Sherry and Paris who are standing along side Monica. "And who are these two lovely ladies?" says Quinton.

Sherry introduces herself and Paris. At that moment Navarro slides into view and catches Paris' eye. They make contact for a second before Paris shyly looks away. "So, what are you ladies doing tonight?" asks Kenneth.

Sherry showing the beginning symptoms of a cold sniffles and responds, "Well it's getting late and me and my girl have to get up early and it is way too cold out here." Paris slowly lifts her head and notices that Navarro is still fixed on her. She smiles a little and tries to look away. Kenneth tries to convince the ladies to stay out with them.

"Come on ladies the night is young let's go eat." he begs. Sherry explains once more. "Its late I have to go to work and my girl has a dance recital to rest for." she nudges Paris on the arm.

Paris quickly lifts her head and responds. "Yes, I have a dance recital." Looking over at Navarro as she responds. Monica tries to gather her pride from off the ground.

"Delray why can't I have a solo?" Delray wastes no time avoids getting into the argument with her. He buttons his coat tips his hat to the girls.

"You ladies have a nice night." He walks away from the group followed by Navarro. Monica stands in disgust as her attempts to sing onstage are disregarded again. Sherry waves goodbye to the guys as they all begin to leave. Paris waves as she looks over at Navarro who is watching her as he walks away. She quietly directs her goodbye to him in a low soft voice.

The ladies begin to walk in the opposite direction and giggle to themselves at how the band members tried so hard to get them to follow. In like fashion members of the Crew comment of the ladies. "Man did you see those eyes." Kenneth says speaking of Paris. "Beautiful."

As Navarro and Delray reach their car Navarro stops and looks back once more. At that moment Paris looks over her shoulder as the two lock eyes.

Paris looks for a quick second before turning away. She puts her head down and smiles thinking to herself maybe her friends are right. Maybe there is something there between the two of them after all.

Navarro pauses for a moment with thoughts in mind that this scene is all too familiar to him. Nonetheless he is intrigued, and that intrigue motivates him to welcome whatever is to come. Sherry sarcastically teases Paris as she notices Paris' distraction.

"So, what do you think now Ms. Paris?" she says. "I saw that eye contact. You know he wants you girl." Paris pauses giving Sherry a very mean look.

"No, he doesn't." She says with a school girlish sense of denial. Monica, not being one to be left out adds her two cents. "Girl please, you know you want him too. If you two were alone, you'd probably be screwing him right now." Paris offended, stops in her tracks. She feverishly stares at Monica while Sherry almost falls to the ground laughing.

"That is so not funny." Paris says with a bit of attitude. Sherry grabs her by the arm, "I'm sorry baby girl you know we are just teasing you. Right Monica?"

Monica hesitates for a moment then responds rolling her eyes. "Yea right." Paris sensing the sarcasm rolls her eyes and brushes Monica off. "Okay, okay I'm sorry." Monica exclaims.

Sherry and Monica both grab Paris by the hand. "We're sorry." Monica says. Paris hesitates but accepts their apology. Though they all reconcile Monica finds another opportunity to get in one last jab. "Besides you need some anyway."

Paris and Sherry stand stunned for a moment before finding the humor in what she has said. The ladies continue down the sidewalk to their vehicles all the while Navarro stands watching from afar.

His eyes stay fixed on Paris as she walks slowly out of sight. He is so fixed that he hasn't heard his grandfather calling to him.

"Navarro, Navarro." Delray calls.

Awakened from his daze he replies. "Yea Pop."

"Um are you going to get in the car son?" Delray gestures he is ready to go.

"Oh, sorry. Yeah I'm coming." Navarro says before glancing down the street once more to catch a glimpse of Paris before she disappears out of sight. He attempts to shake off this feeling and gets in the car.

Closing the door as he sits down, he still can't help but to wonder if he will see her again. The car pulls away from the curb as Delray reaches down to turn on the radio. The sound of Flamenco Sketches by Miles Davis floats through the air. Slowly the cold air within gives way to the warmth from the car's heater as it soothes both of them.

Finding peace within in the music Navarro leans back in his seat and closes his eyes. If only for a second, he wishes to relax but he cannot for his mind is consumed with thoughts of the one he just met. Fighting this feeling does no good so he gives way to his thoughts. He leans further back and thinks to himself, "There's always tomorrow..."

14

The Light of Morning

THE LIGHT OF MORNING brings a refreshing wind. The chaotic sound of traffic and the railway cars all come to a stand still as the singing of birds becomes accented by the sound of Beethoven coming from Delray's home.

Within the study Navarro sits at the piano. He sits focused, playing each note with such intensity that everything around him becomes a blank canvas. His grandfather stands in the kitchen listening as he makes breakfast for the two of them.

As Navarro plays harder, he suddenly feels the pain of another migraine coming on. The pounding of the headache seems to increase his efforts of play. With each key that he strikes his pain becomes stronger and more intense. He tries to continue until the pain becomes so unbearable that he stops playing to rub his forehead while resting his elbow on the piano. He closes his eyes only to be struck by a vision of his mother being violently attacked. The sound of her scream rings aloud as his vision quickly disappears. He opens his eyes, wondering what has just happened as he wipes his face and takes a moment to gather his thoughts.

Suddenly he notices a drop of blood on the piano. He looks down to investigate moving his finger across the piano at that moment another drop of blood falls, quickly followed by another. The bright red color of his blood stands out against the pure white keys of the piano.

As he lifts his head and touches his nose the sight of blood startles him as he quickly wipes his face with a nearby towel. His grandfather, hearing nothing from the study has come to investigate. He quickly appears behind Navarro. "Why did you stop playing? What happened" Delray asks.

Navarro quickly turns his back to hide the towel covered in blood from his grandfather. "Oh um, nothing Pop. I just took a break for a minute," he says.

Dropping the towel to the floor he quickly kicks it to the side of the piano out of view from Delray. Growing a little suspicious Delray becomes inquisitive.

"Is everything alright?" he asks.

Navarro wipes his face again to make sure no blood remains.

"Yeah Pop everything's ok. I'm okay." he says as he turns to Delray. Moving in closer to investigate Delray asks again. "Are you sure you're okay?"

"Yes, sir everything's cool. I'm good. Nothing to worry about" Navarro tells him. Delray pauses for a second before letting go of his suspicions.

"Well why did you stop playing? You know I like to hear you play while I make breakfast." he says, while placing his hand on Navarro's shoulder.

Navarro looks up at him and smiles. "I know that Pop."

Delray turns to the door, before exiting he says "Well its okay, its time for breakfast anyway. Come on and eat."

Navarro looks down at his watch to take note of the time. "I can't this morning Pop I have to go downtown for a meeting with the symphony to go over the set list for the show."

Delray turns back to him. "Uh-huh, and what time do you have to be there?" Looking at his watch again Navarro answers. "In about an hour."

"Great!" Delray exclaims, "That's plenty of time come eat young blood."

Navarro shrugs his shoulders, as there's no sense in arguing he will never get his way so reluctantly he agrees.

"Okay old man, I'm coming."

Delray walks out of the room and from the kitchen he yells. "Besides you need to eat, you look a little frail. You can't focus on an empty stomach no way."

Navarro looks himself over and says quietly under his breath. "Oh my God, you cooked, now I know I'm in trouble."

Delray yells from the kitchen. "I heard that!"

Navarro smiles as he gets up from the piano. Forgetting what he has just remembered from his past, inadvertently he suppresses his thoughts deep within his mind. Acting quickly to dispose of the towel covered in blood he reaches down behind the piano to scoop it up. Swiftly he folds the towel and carries it to his bedroom to hide it deep within his clothes hamper.

Taking a moment to gather himself he stares at his image in the mirror. With a slight sense of what has just happened he shakes off his feelings and puts on another face. One he has used so many times when facing something unknown. He removes his feelings from it and carries on as if it never existed.

After a few more moments his grandfather calls to him again. "Navarro, come on son."

Navarro yells back. "I'm coming pop."

Before leaving his room, he looks once more at himself in the mirror. From the corner of his eye something grabs his attention. A photo stands out on his dresser.

He takes a second to focus on the photo, one of him and his mother at a happier time. He walks over to the photo grabbing it from the dresser he uses his hand to examine the frame. Sliding his fingers against the glass slowly outlining the photo of his mother and a younger version of himself.

Removing the dust from the glass almost seemingly to caress his mother face, his affection for her is shown in how he keeps the photo close to his chest. Taking in a deep breath then releasing a sigh he places the photo gently back in its place on the dresser. He closes his eyes and lowers his head as if to pray but saying no words. Something he has locked away for so long he fights away with his silence. The feelings of his past he has come to control by simply forgetting. Only reminded of his past by the very photo in front of him. He cannot forget all, as he wants to honor the memory of his mother and what she has meant to him.

He stands for a few seconds before rushing out of the room to join his grandfather for breakfast. Before leaving he looks back at the photo for one last glance. He then turns off the light and pulls the door gently closed as if it helps to close a chapter within his life that cannot be forgotten. Nonetheless he tries. He tries to forget the hurt and pain of his past, while still remembering his mother in a loving and caring light.

Success in doing so over the years has not brought him to a place of calm as he thinks, it has only calmed the volcano within him, as he has not fully addressed the feelings that have been allowed to fester and lay dormant for so many years. But as many things do, they will soon come to pass as all things will at some point have their day in the light after l so long in the dark.

15

Love's Melody

THE CITY IS ALIVE. Thousands flood the downtown area some for business some for pleasure. Crowds fill the many café's and shops as well as business districts all for different purposes. In the center of downtown stands a huge theatre hall used to display concerts, plays and symphonies.

While the city is buzzing outside things are just as busy inside. Navarro meets with the orchestra conductor to discuss the upcoming symphony performance he has written and will display for thousands in just a few weeks.

The conductor, Mr. Perry is a gray-haired chubby man with a heavy English accent. As the meeting between he and Navarro concludes the two of them walk through the theatre foyer and go over the final plans for the show.

"So now that everything is in place, all we need is that beautiful mind of yours and your newest composition. I can't wait to hear it." Mr. Perry says with an enthusiastic nature.

Navarro pauses for a moment. His pause leaves question in Mr. Perry's mind about the completion of the work. "It is completed isn't it?" He asks.

Speaking quickly to prevent further questioning, Navarro responds. "Yeah, its finished. It's ready to go."

Bringing a smile to Mr. Perry's face, he oozes with excitement. "Great, now we must rehearse the close of the show soon. We have only three weeks until curtains up. Everything must be tight."

Navarro shakes his head in agreement. "Yes, I know, all will be fine. It will be ready," he says.

As the two of them continue to walk they pass by the entry door to the auditorium. The sound of a dance rehearsal comes from inside. Navarro vaguely notices what he thinks is Paris onstage. Mr. Perry continues to speak all the while Navarro is totally focused on what is going on in the auditorium. His curiosity draws him closer.

Taking notice to what Navarro has just said Mr. Perry grows concerned. "Will be ready? What do you mean, will be ready? Is it ready or isn't it?" he asks.

Navarro stares into the auditorium paying no attention to Mr. Perry. "Mr. Navarro, do you hear me?" he asks.

Navarro turns to him for a second snapping out of his daze. "Huh, yes. Yes, I hear you. Look don't worry okay. All will be fine."

Navarro then turns his attention to the stage again. Mr. Perry continues to discuss the coming events. "Good, I can't wait to hear it. If the end is as good as the opening, we are in for quite a treat."

Growing tired of watching from the hallway, Navarro wants to venture closer. Eager to find out if that was indeed the girl, he saw the other night at his show. He begins to hurry the conductor with good-byes so that he may leave.

Hurriedly he says. "Hey, um I will catch up with you next week to go over any changes that may be needed." Navarro then rushes into the auditorium quietly, as the conductor stands behind shouting out his last remarks.

Yelling from the foyer he says. "Okay, hey don't forget to bring your composition."

Shaking his head and walking to the exit he says speaking of Navarro. "That's a strange fellow, but again the great ones always are."

Upon entering the auditorium Navarro is pleasantly surprised to find that in fact it is Paris on stage. He chooses a seat in back of the auditorium as to not disturb anyone while they are practicing.

Center stage the dance instructor is lecturing a class of 10 dancers on the importance of focus while performing. She's a middle aged African American woman standing roughly 5 feet 1 inch in height. While giving her lecture she begins to critique the ladies in her class as they perform their routine. A mixture of modern dance and classical ballet, the women struggle through the move's as they are very difficult to perform.

The instructor growing tired of the lackluster performance begins to bellow out instructions. "Ladies you have to be fluid. Your movements should flow like water." She yells out at them slapping her hands with each word.

Reaching her boiling point, she halts the performance. "Okay everyone stop! I want all eyes on me. Some of you are not showing me anything. I see that most of you don't want to be here" she screams.

The ladies all simultaneously come to a stand still. They form a circle around the instructor to watch as she demonstrates the routine.

"This is how you should perform." She explains. "You should move with some meaning, not all over the stage."

After she performs the routine the scolding continues. "Now what is the problem, this is a big opportunity for some of you and you are blowing it". Again, with rapid succession slapping her hands together with each word.

The ladies all stand in silence with their eyes fixed on their feet as to not make eye contact with the instructor.

"If you do not want to be here then leave. Otherwise show me some intensity. Show me you want this." She pleads.

The ladies continue to stand quiet. Some begin to look around at one another the rest hold their heads down. They have a look of school children standing in a circle with an anxious look on their faces, all drenched in sweat dressed in leotards and ballet shoes.

The instructor surveys the crowd of girls looking for someone to call out to center stage. Her eyes scan over the group once, then once more before landing on Paris. "Paris!" She calls ecstatically.

Paris jumps wiping sweat from her face she stands shocked to be called of all people. Shyly she replies. "Yes ma'am?"

The instructor walks closer to her, nose to nose she asks. "Why are you here?" Paris, a little confused by the questions takes a step back. The instructor asks again, "Why are you here?"

Paris takes a moment to gather her thoughts. Navarro sits in the back of the auditorium very intrigued by what he sees. He sits up in his chair crossing his arms and resting them on the seat in front of him.

"Ladies I need you all to know why it is that you are here. If you do not know, no one else will." The instructor explains.

The group of women stand fixed on her. The instructor reaches out her hand. "Paris comes forward." she says.

Paris walks to center stage. As she does the instructor tells the rest of the ladies to stand back. As the women move back one after the other, the instructor grabs Paris by the hand and looks her in the eye. "Show me why you are here." she says softly yet with determination.

Paris stands a little embarrassed to be called out in front of the group but nonetheless she is up for the task. The instructor calls to the sound booth for the music to start. She turns to Paris once more and says to her. "Show me why you're here. Show me why I should pick you."

Paris takes a deep breath and nods her head. Everyone including the dance instructor backs away as the sound of renaissance music plays from the huge overhead speaker system. Navarro leans even further in his chair in anticipation of what is about to happen.

The music flows softly as Paris begins to move. She slowly moves her arms accenting the curvature of her body. From her hips to her breast then lips, her hands move gently caressing her frame. With a loud bang the music explodes as she gracefully performs. Giving off electrifying energy she moves from one end of the stage to the next.

She glides through the air with every pirouette more graceful than the first. Navarro watches in awe as Paris delivers a powerful performance. Her sleek movements form a silhouette of beauty. His eyes can't believe how beautiful she looks.

As quickly as it began her performance comes to a close, she lands the entire piece. Flawless in her efforts the crowd of women explodes with cheer and applause including the dance instructor who is impressed by what she has just witnessed.

The ladies all come over and pat Paris on the back, as does the dance instructor giving her a hug and whispering in her ear. "You're in."

Paris smiles with shock and amazement. "I'm in?" she asks with disbelief.

The instructor nods her head in confirmation that yes Paris has made it. Elated Paris grabs the dance instructor hugging her tightly around the neck. "Thank you, thank you, thank you so much." she says emphatically.

Navarro impressed by what he has seen as well, smiles before quickly exiting the auditorium as to keep anyone from noticing him. As he leaves Paris looks out at the empty auditorium as if she felt someone there but didn't see.

In a rush the dancers surround Paris giving her hugs and congratulations on her performance. Getting back to the matter of business the instructor interrupts to direct the lady's attention on rehearsal. "Ladies, ladies okay that's enough. Let's get back into formation. Lord knows some of you till need work."

The women quickly rush to get in order to reach their places. Paris still overwhelmed by the idea of making the group stands her body exploding with energy and excitement with a huge smile on her face.

She tries to gather herself before getting in line. Before doing so she takes one more look out into the auditorium sure that she felt someone there. In the dark sea of chairs, she surveys every one of them. Seeing no one she turns her attention to the instructor. Trying to calm the storm of excitement within her she stands poised to learn more. Alas this is the beginning of her dream. Something she has long waited for has finally come to fruition.

16

They Meet Again

THE SUN SHINES BRIGHT. Navarro stands outside the auditorium against the huge columns forming the base for the giant statues that decorate the front of the building. He stands patiently waiting for Paris to exit the building.

Curiosity has grown within him. So much so that he has found the courage to finally inquire about this woman that has been immersed within his thoughts since he first laid eyes on her. As the time drags on, he repeatedly looks down at his watch wondering, will she ever come out if this building.

Moments later the front doors of the theatre swing open and a flood of women pour out. Navarro peers through the crowd of women looking for Paris. Suddenly she appears and his heart pounds against his chest. With her back to him and eyes to the pavement she walks in the opposite direction making quick steps, as she is still excited about her audition.

Navarro quickly moves in behind her. Saying only one word he grabs her attention. "Congratulations." Paris stops, thinking to herself "That voice is familiar".

She lifts her head and smiles before turning to face him. Flustered she replies back. "Hi, um thank you. How did you?" It dawns on her. "So, it was you out watching," she says. "I thought I saw someone there"

"I enjoyed your dance". Navarro says. "It was very nice." Paris shy, trying hard not to make eye contact with him only says. "Thank you."

The two of them stand in silence for a brief second before Navarro opens the conversation. "So, you're Paris, right?" he asks.

Jokingly Paris throws back, "Yes and you are?"

Navarro shows a cocky smile, as he knows she definitely remembers his name. Yet he still answers. "Ah, yes my name is Navarro."

He reaches his hand out to take hers for a formal handshake. Paris shakes his hand and admits "I was just joking I know who you are. I saw you perform the other night. Your performance was nice also."

Navarro smiles in appreciation. "So, it was nice huh?" he asks.

Paris responds back "Yes, very nice."

Noticing Navarro is still holding her hand she nervously let's go and changes subjects.

"So, do you always wait around outside theatres to meet women?" she asks with a smile.

Navarro gives in to her question and responds back. "No, I had a little business inside."

Paris inquires a little more "What business?" she asks.

Navarro shyly maneuvers around the question. "Just a little business."

Taking the hint Paris knows she's not going to get much out of him, so she drops the question.

Suddenly it happens. "So, what are you about to do?" Navarro asks.

Taking a moment to answer Paris says, "Well I was about to go to Café Andre. "Café Andre?" Navarro responds. "Well if you don't mind, I will join you."

Taken by the forward nature of Navarro, Paris quickly answers.

"No, I mean yes." she says stumbling over her words. She takes a moment to gather herself. Calmly she says, "I meant yes, I would like it if you joined me."

Navarro takes a moment to confirm her acceptance. "Are you sure?" he asks. "Yes, yes I'm sure." She says with a coy smile on her face.

In a rush Navarro moves toward his car. "Well let's go." he directs.

Remembering she has just left a dance rehearsal and needs to freshen up Paris stops him. "Wait I have to change clothes first. It will only take a second. I will meet you there in 10 minutes."

Navarro takes a moment to survey her with his eyes. Seeing nothing wrong with how she looks from his point of view, but he understands she may want to get out of her dance cloths, so he reluctantly agrees. "Okay 10 minutes. I will meet you there."

Paris rushes off, but before she does, she commits again to meeting Navarro. "Okay, I promise I won't have you waiting too long." she says.

Navarro smile and watches as Paris hurries off. He keeps his eyes locked on her as she navigates her way down the steps leading to the street where her car is parked.

Before getting in her car she smiles and waves at him. Navarro instantly sees a vision from his past, a feeling of deja vu, as if this scene has played out before. In a flash his surroundings change. His vision becomes reality.

He sees himself standing in the schoolyard as a child watching his friend Melanie wave goodbye to him. One of many feelings and memories he has buried deep within over the years has come to the surface. As soon as it comes to him in a flash it disappears. He quickly snaps out of it. He wonders where that image came from.

Unbeknownst to him that he has a lot of repressed memories locked away inside. He watches Paris for a moment before turning and walking away brushing aside what he has just remembered. A unique gift he has come to master over the years in dealing with his feelings and his past.

17

Café Andre

THE MORNING TURNS TO AFTERNOON. Navarro sits alone in Café Andre waiting for Paris to arrive. He sits near the front of the café peering out of the window. Searching for the inspiration to complete his unfinished work he blocks out all background noise and focuses on the sheet music on the table in front of him. The sounds of traffic slowly turn from incoherent noise to a complex rhythm for him.

The noises give way to subtle notes of music. One after the next they come together as he looks down and translating his thoughts to paper. At that moment he glances out of the window and sees Paris walking the sidewalk leading to the café. He watches as she moves each step more graceful than the next. Divinity in motion, sure grace as she enters the café.

Navarro watches as her appearance strangely transforms into a vision of his mother. He frame appears, her smile, her hair her very being coming toward him.

His heart begins to pound feverishly. He loses his breath, as he can't believe what he is seeing. Shocked he closes his eyes to gather himself. He opens them just as Paris steps in front of him. Paris taps Navarro on the shoulder. Taking off her jacket she sits at the table with him. "I'm sorry I'm late." she says.

Pulling her seat closer to the table. Navarro sitting with a stoic look on his face sits in silence. "Is everything ok?" Paris asks with a look of concern. "You haven't been waiting long, have you?"

Navarro shakes his mood and turns all attention to her. "I'm fine." he says. "I haven't been waiting too long."

Navarro stares at Paris. Her dark eyes so hypnotic draws him in entrancing him. Paris pauses for a moment. "What's wrong?" she says.

Navarro just stares becoming lost in her eyes. A second seems to last forever before he answers. "Nothing, nothings wrong. You look nice."

The compliment brings a schoolgirl blush to Paris' cheeks. She returns the compliment with a simple "thank you". After the exchange Paris looks down at the table and notices the composition

Navarro has been working on. She leans in closer to get a better look.

"What are you working on?' she asks with intrigue.

Navarro being very protective of his work simply replies. "Its nothing." Not convinced Paris asks again. "Nothing huh, come on tell me."

Navarro thinks to himself for a moment "Should I?" The look on Paris' face lets him know that she will not give up on the question, so he gives in.

"Okay, but it isn't completed yet." he tells her. She reassures him that all is ok. "It's fine, just let me see."

Navarro pauses. "Okay, but can you read sheet music?" sliding the composition across the table to her.

She picks it up and her minimal knowledge of music composition isn't enough to understand the complexity of what he has written. With a bewildered look on her face she reluctantly places the composition back on the table.

"Maybe you can read it to me." she says to him. Surprised by the question. One that has never been asked of him Navarro reaches his hand out to receive the sheet music.

"You want me to read it to you?" he asks.

"Yes, would you?" Paris replies.

Navarro accepts her invitation and moves his chair around the table closer to hers. He grabs the sheet music and begins explaining the instruments and notes that make up each scale. Paris leans in closer to him and listens intensely. In a low mellow tone, he explains.

"The beginning starts simple just a simple sounding oboe. Then comes a flute accenting the oboe."

He stops for a moment and turns to Paris. She sits with a look of being just as lost as if she were reading the composition herself.

Navarro calmly asks, "Do you understand?"

Paris shyly replies "Um, no. I'm sorry."
Navarro leans back in his chair for a second. Quickly he comes up with a way to help Paris better understand the music.
He looks at her, "Close your eyes." he directs.

Paris just looks at him with a look that say's "What does he have in mind." Again, he tells her "Close your eyes."

She looks him in the eye as he stares back at her. "Trust me." he says to her softly. Without saying a word, she slowly closes her eyes. The smile on her face is erased as he moves closer to her, giving way to a little apprehension on her part. She doesn't know what to expect.

He moves in close, placing his mouth near her ear. Utilizing a much different approach to explain the beauty of what's written on the sheet in front of her. He whispers in her ear.

"Picture a lake surrounded by mountains. Still waters encompassed by trees, the leaves different shades." Paris inadvertently replies "okay."

Navarro quickly quiets her. "Shhh, just listen" he says as he begins again.

"There are no birds singing. There's no wind blowing only silence. The night is clear, and the moon is full. Can you picture it?"

Paris nods her head to acknowledge the vision. Navarro continues.

"Your standing by the water as it begins to rain. The drops slowly fall. One by one hitting the ground making the same thumping sound. Sounds like an oboe. Gently repeating, over and over moderately fast."

Suddenly a sound begins to play in Paris' mind creating a sense of serenity. All other sounds are drowned out but the sound of Navarro's voice in her ear. Navarro moves even closer his lips nearly touching her cheek. His whisper becomes more intense.

"The rain brings a slight rumbling of thunder. A soft rumble as it accompanies the warmth of the rain. Like that of a string section creating the background of a song."

Navarro's hand slowly grabs hold of Paris' hand. She gives a subtle smile, but her eyes remain closed.

"Suddenly the wind begins to blow." Navarro says in a low breathy tone.

"Soft at first, gentle to the touch but strong in breath. A breath that seems to last forever. A light tone of a flute personifies this wind."

Navarro opens Paris' hand and gently moves his finger across her palm.

"Imagine the wind gliding across the lake creating ripples within the water. The sound begins to waver but still strong as it carries on."

He moves his finger from her palm to her forearm, seductively caressing her arm as he explains. She flinches anxiously with each touch.

Seductively he asks, "Can you here?" Paris doesn't reply she just nods as she begins to feel the effects of his seduction. Listening closely to his voice the song grows stronger and louder in her mind.

Moving from her cheek to her lips the warmth of his breath she can feel against her lips. Although her eyes are closed, she can feel that he is very close. As he speaks, she makes a move closer to him. His voice becomes her guide through a universe she has never traveled. Every word she hangs to as if not to let go otherwise she will be left behind alone lost in a vast space she has never traveled.

He continues to speak to her in a whisper "The thunder grows stronger and nearer as the wind blows harder. Suddenly the two collide."

Navarro reaches his hand to touch Paris' face. No longer startled by his touch she opens her eyes. As she does, he looks back at her. They lock eyes and stare deep within drawn to each other, gravity pulling them closer together.

The world between the two of them stands no longer distant as their worlds are now joined together. Navarro looks her deep in the eye and continues to speak.

"Not a clash but a mixture of sound and wind." he says. "The two delicately wound together. Natures way of making love."

They draw closer to one another with each word spoken. Just a breath away their lips almost meet. Seconds seem like an eternity as they stare at one another. Waiting for their cue to join lips they sit in silence. Each wait on the other to make the first move.

Suddenly the café waitress interrupts them. They quickly separate as their journey comes to an end. "Hi, are you ready to order?" the waitress asks in a loud and very quirky voice. Paris shyly recoils in her seat and gathers herself.

"Yes, I will have a chocolate and cream latte" she says to the waitress. The waitress turns to Navarro who still has his eyes fixed on Paris.

"No thank you. Nothing for me." he says. The waitress writing down the order confirms before retreating behind the counter. Paris sits quiet with her head down her hands in her lap. Her silence is broken as she addresses what has just happened.

"That sounds beautiful" she says.

Navarro looks her in the eye without warning. "You're beautiful" he says reaching on the table to gather his composition. Paris smiles, lowers her head, and moves closer to him.

"So where did you learn how to do all that? To play music I mean." she asks. Navarro thinks to himself for a moment before totally avoiding the question.

"Hey, let's get out of here?" he says. Paris looks around for the waitress.

"Right now? What about my latte?" Navarro grabs her hand and stands up from the table. "Come on, I want to show you something." he says hurriedly and with a bit of excitement.

At that moment the waitress returns with Paris' drink. "Here you are, enjoy." Paris takes the drink and sips once then once more. Navarro pulls on her again. "Come on let's go. Bring it with you" he says.

Paris once again apprehensive about his actions knowing that this is in fact their first one on one. She wonders what he could possibly have to show her. Nonetheless she shakes her feeling and slides out of her chair to her feet. "Okay" she says much to Navarro's delight.

Navarro helps her with her jacket as they walk toward the door.

"This better be good." Paris exclaims. "You do know it's cold out there, right." Navarro says nothing just leads her out of the café. As they reach the door Paris stops him. "Wait." she says.

Navarro looks back at her before opening the door. "What, what's wrong?" he asks.

Paris looks him in the eye and leans forward to kiss him on the cheek before exiting the café. "Nothing, nothings wrong." she says with a smile. She then walks out of the café leaving Navarro standing with a smile on his face and just a little surprised.

He quickly shakes the feeling of surprise before exiting after her. Grabbing her by the hand he leads her to his car. He quickly helps her get in and closes the door evident he is eager to share what he has in store for her. His feeling mirrored by that of Paris as she anxiously awaits this surprise. Navarro jumps in the driver's seat and closes the door. Quickly starts the car and off they go. Again, the worlds that were so far apart a few days ago are now aligned with a strong sense of gravity pulling the two together.

18

The Loft

THE COLD INHABITS the huge loft space used by
Navarro and the band for rehearsals. It's very dark and cold devoid
of any sound.

Suddenly the noise of an elevator begins to sound off
loudly as it reaches the loft floor coming to a stop. Only a small
overhead light illuminates the space surrounding the elevator. In
the dark a voice is heard. "This is it." Navarro says leading Paris to
the front of the elevator.

The elevator stops and Navarro lifts the huge metal bars
that act as a door for the elevator to exit. They step out into the
huge room the only thing that can be seen is the overhead light

from the elevator. The dark seems to go on forever as if they are lost in space.

Paris takes note of her surroundings. "Oh my God its cold and dark in here." She says trying to keep her teeth from rattling together and warming herself by rubbing her hands against her arms.

Navarro tries to calm her concerns by grabbing her hand. "Just follow me, I'm right here" he says.

They walk toward the wall adjacent to the elevator as Navarro turns on the lights revealing the massive loft space and the instruments decorating it.

"There, is that better?" Navarro asks. Paris surveys the room and just nods her head. She takes note of all the instruments littering the room.

"I'll be back. I'm going to turn the heat on." Navarro says. This is surely music to the ears of Paris as she stands shivering from the cold. Navarro leaves her to herself as he walks behind a huge wall disappearing from view. Paris stands for a moment then ventures off to investigate her surroundings.

She walks by the rehearsal area and admires the many instruments lying around. Testing a microphone, she playfully attempts to see if it works by blowing into it. Just as he disappeared, Navarro re-appears joining Paris by the rehearsal area.

"It should get better in a minute." he tells her. Paris acknowledges him by nodding her head and again rubbing her arms trying to warm herself. She looks around the room again and asks. "So, who plays all of these instruments?" Navarro looks around for a moment before answering. "I do."

Paris stands somewhat in shock by what he has said. Amazed she can't believe that one person could be capable of playing so many instruments.

"So, you play all of these?" she asks.

Navarro responds. "Yes, I do, why what's wrong?" Silent for a moment she takes a second to formulate exactly what she means to say.

"Its just seems a little amazing that's all." Navarro takes her compliment and returns in kind.

"Well your dancing is amazing." Paris takes the compliment almost in disbelief. "My dancing is nothing like this" she says. "You play all of these I could only wish to be a great dancer as you are a musician."

Navarro moves closer to her and moves her hair away from her face. "You are a great dancer. Not everyone can do what you do it is wonderful."

Paris holds her head low and smiles. "Thank you." she says before moving closer to the microphone again. She then remembers there was a reason he brought her to this place. What is it he wants he to see? She asks, "So where is this surprise you had to show me?"

Navarro reaches out his hand. "Come with me." he says. She takes his hand as they make their way around another huge wall revealing another open area, where in the center of the room something sits covered in a huge dark drape.

"This is it." Navarro says. Paris looks at him with a blank stare.

"Okay, a car cover." She says sarcastically.

"No not, well let me show you." Navarro says. He grabs a corner of the huge drapery and pulls it off. Underneath sits a bold grand piano. A polished ivory white shade of wood remarkably sparkles underneath the loft's huge lights. Paris stands speechless as her eyes survey the huge beautiful piano.

"Do you like it?" Navarro asks. Paris takes a moment to breathe. She moves closer to the piano gently running her hand down the side of it.

"Yes, it is beautiful." She says. She makes her way around to the front of the piano. Her fingers tease the keys softly. She turns to Navarro with a look of anticipation.

"Will you play it for me?" she asks him. He walks closer to her.

"Sure, sit next to me." he tells her. The two sits down at the piano. Navarro's eyes fixed on the piano keys while Paris has her eyes fixed on him.

"What would you like to hear?" he asks.

"Play anything you want to play." she responds. Navarro looks at her then down at the piano for a moment before replying.

"I'll play something about you." Paris looks at him and smiles. "Okay."

As he readies his fingers with strategic placement, Paris sits in anticipation of what Navarro will play. As he begins, she moves closer to him. Infatuated with his play and his voice she finds herself becoming more and more intrigued by him. The piano then comes to life as Navarro sings.

"I get lost within the thoughts of mine, looking deep within your eyes. And there's no fear because I see you there. And every time I dream, we are whispering words that only you and I can hear. And if I can't have your heart, girl I couldn't live if I had to breathe without you."

The words strike a chord in Paris' heart. As Navarro sings, she falls deeper and deeper into his every word. Once he stops and the last note is played, she looks him deep in the eye. Closer and closer they move together until they are centimeters from one another.

Their lips finally touch. A soft slow gentle kiss captured within a few moments seems to last forever. They separate assessing what has just happened, what they have just shared. No words are needed as they speak mentally, emotionally, affectionately.

Their eyes call to one another as they find themselves again moving closer together. A single moment passes before their lips reunite. A deeper kiss ensues as Navarro gently touches her cheek. Paris wraps her arms around his waist pulling herself closer to him. So many words to say between the two yet delivered with just a kiss.

Before things get even more intense the two separates. Navarro looks at Paris and she at him as if to agree that its time to go. A rush to bed with one another should not ruin the beauty of this night.

Navarro grabs Paris by the hand. "Come, I will take you back." Paris slowly stands and agrees. They both walk toward the exit not saying a word before disappearing into the elevator. The awkward distance between the two is noticeable but yet they both have this burning desire growing within, wanting more.

The afternoon gives way to the sunset of evening. A slight bit of traffic fills the downtown streets. After leaving the loft Navarro takes Paris back to her car. He pulls in front of Café Andre and slowly stops along side Paris' car.

As the car stops Paris glances out of the window before turning to Navarro to comment on their day together. "I really had a nice time with you tonight." she says.

Navarro turns to her and smiles. "So, did I, thank you." They hold hands for a second while sitting in silence.

"Well I guess I should go now." Paris says.

"Okay, you're right." Navarro replies. Paris slowly motions toward the door, moving with a snail's pace as if she wants to say something more.

Before she can get a foot out the door Navarro stops her. "Hey so um, what are you doing tomorrow night?" he asks.

Paris stops and turns to him with a smile. "Nothing, well I have rehearsal but after that I'm free." she says.

"Come by the club tomorrow night I want to play something for you." he tells her. Paris thinks it over for a moment then agrees to come. "What time should I be there?" she asks.

"I go on at nine." he says. She again agrees to come and moves toward the door. "Wait!" He says stopping her from going.

She turns to him slowly. "You forgot something." he says before leaning over and kissing her softly on the lips. The kiss lasts more than a few seconds as Paris' hand slowly finds its place against Navarro's cheek caressing it gently. After their kiss they stare at one another and smile. Paris wipes the lipstick she was wearing from Navarro's lips then kisses him once more.

"Goodbye, I will see you tomorrow" she says to him before getting out of the car. She turns to him before unlocking her cars door and getting in. She waves and says goodbye once more. He smiles and waves before driving off.

Paris watches as he pulls away. Before starting her car, she sits and reflects on what just happened. She brandishes a huge smile before shaking it off. Recounting the events of the night she quickly grabs her purse to reach for her cell phone to call her girls. Before dialing she pauses and thinks to herself maybe she shouldn't say anything. She knows her friends can be very critical of her and her movements. She thinks it over for a second before deciding that this secret will be one that is held between her and Navarro. She will keep this one close to her until it is time to reveal what has happened.

She brandishes a huge smile and grabs the collar of the jacket she was wearing to place it under her nose. She breathes in deeply taking in the scent of Navarro, the cologne he was wearing still leaving its mark against her clothing. She takes one more breath before exhaling. She soon comes down from her emotional high and focuses on heading home. She starts her car and pulls away with her heart still pounding excited about this new feeling that has taken over her. Strange but true, she surely welcomes it.

19

Dreams

NIGHTMARES FILL HIS DREAMS. Navarro lies asleep in bed tossing. Sweat running down his face he is haunted by his dreams. He dreams of himself at age 10 standing in the kitchen doorway of his home watching his mother being beaten by her boyfriend. He wants to help her, but he can't. His little feet won't move. The more and more his mother cries out to him the more he tries to move.

Motionless he can do nothing else but scream. He yells from the top of his lungs. "Stop!" The screeching of his voice makes Wayne turn from his mother and toward his direction. The look on Wayne's face is frightening. He charges Navarro, cursing him. "I'll fucking kill you too!" he screams at Navarro.

Navarro's little body stands trembling. With every step Wayne moves closer to him. He feels the vibration under his little feet. Closer and closer Wayne moves in. Navarro attempts to move again but can't. He stands there and closes his eyes bracing for the impact blow from Wayne. Wayne reaches him and draws back to strike.

As Navarro opens his eyes wide showing fear, Karen yells out. "No! Leave him alone!"

Suddenly Navarro awakes leaping from his bed reaching out to his mother.

Sitting erect in bed with his heart pounding and breathing heavy, he wipes the sweat from his forehead as he takes a moment to calm down. He leans over and turns on a lamp adjacent to his bed. Taking another moment to collect his thoughts, for the first time he realizes that he can no longer hide from the past that haunts him.

Wiping the sweat from his face he glances over to the nightstand sitting next to his bed. He notices a picture of his mother and himself as a child. He stares for a moment accepting that his past has finally caught up to him. He lies back against his pillow and looks up at the ceiling. Totally not in the mood for going back to sleep he gets out of bed and puts on his robe before walking out of his bedroom.

He walks from his bedroom into the hallway leading to his grandfather's room. The dimly lit walls are decorated with the many photos of past musicians his grandfather admires. Stopping for a moment he examines some of the photos. Soon after he creeps down the hallway toward his grandfather's room. Once he reaches it, he gently opens the door to find his grandfather asleep in his recliner, papers littering his lap.

Navarro walks over to his grandfather and gently removes his reading glasses and the papers from his lap. He takes a heavy blanket from his grandfathers' bed and covers him with it. He rubs his Delray's' head as if he wants to say something to him, but he does not. Navarro kneels down next to his grandfather and just stares at him for a moment. He surveys Delray's face noticing the years of hard work imprinted by the many wrinkles it contains.

Soon his attention becomes drawn to the papers he is holding. Apparent it seems his grandfather has been working on a composition of his own. Intrigued Navarro investigates the work further. He slowly takes the papers from his Delray's lap and slips it under his arm. He gently gets up from the floor and tiptoes out of the room as to not wake his grandfather. He navigates his way down the hall back to his bedroom. Upon reaching his room he gently shuts the door behind him.

Placing the composition on the bed he quickly finds the order of the arrangement and looks it over. A simple title sits atop the page it reads "*Immersion*". Composed around a piano and nothing more it's a slow piece very melodic somewhat simple it is however complex. His eyes take in every note. He moves from one scale to the next playing the composition in his mind. He covers the entire piece before stopping. He looks wondering what his grandfather must've been thinking in order to create such a piece.

It is somewhat somber yet moving with a deliberate sense of pace and urgency. What is he trying to say he wonders?

Navarro has been taught everything by his grandfather, yet he is amazed by the work his grandfather has done. He takes a moment to admire the piece of work once more. All these years past and his grandfather is still teaching him how to convey his emotion and feeling through his work.

While admiring the work his eyes survey his room. He stops when they come across the picture of himself and his mother. He pauses for a moment. He looks at the photo then down at the composition. He thinks for a moment could this be the inspiration.

As to not disturb the work any further he quickly places the pages back in order and slips out of his room down the hall to his grandfather's room. He slowly opens the door and peeks inside. Noticing his grandfather is still asleep he places the composition back on his lap then swiftly turns to exit the room. Before closing the door, he peers in once more. Again, so much to say but the words cannot escape him. He closes the door then makes the walk back to his room. He walks with his head down until he reaches his room. He goes inside and disappears behind the door as it closes slowly behind him.

He jumps in his bed and folds his pillow behind his head. He looks up at the ceiling staring into space. He closes his eyes and attempts to drift back to sleep. As his eyes close, he again hears the sound of music. This time it is not his own. It is the music of his grandfather.

20

A New Song

THE MUSIC IS EXPLOSIVE as a massive crowd gathers outside of Club Epiphany waiting in line to enter. Women dressed in their best as well as the men all have come to witness another showing by Navarro.

The club is packed with men and women of all ages desperately trying to find the best tables and seats in the house. On stage Papa D and The Crew perform a jazz montage filled with blistering horns and funky guitar riffs, blending the genres of Jazz, Pop, and Rhythm and Blues. As his grandfather sings, Navarro watches from the side of the stage admiring the showmanship of Delray. He is impressed by his grandfather's ability to hold a crowd and move on stage at his age.

As Navarro watches a bouncer walks up behind him. "Papa looks good tonight" he says to Navarro. "You better watch out before he takes your spot."

Navarro looks at him and doesn't say a word. He just turns back to the stage and watches in admiration. Soon after his attention is drawn to a figure, he notices that has just walked in the door. From the side of the stage he sees Paris enter the room.

Dressed in a tight fitted burgundy dress she peers through the club looking for a seat before settling for a place at the bar. As she walks to the bar, she sees her friend Monica already planted at the bar flirting with the bar tender. Monica sits deep in a flirtatious mood trying to temp the bartender into giving her a free drink. Paris creeps up slowly from behind to surprise Monica. She gets within a few inches of her and peers over her shoulder. Monica doesn't notice as she is relishing over the free drink she has just received from the bar.

After a second sip of her drink she finally turns around and at that instant notices Paris leaning over her should. Startled she spills the drink nearly getting it all over her dress. "Oh my God! Damn you scared the shit out of me girl" she screams at Paris.

Apologetically Paris responds. "Oh, I am so sorry."

Monica takes a minute to calm down surveying her outfit she makes sure that nothing has been spilt on it. "Girl its okay." she says. "The bad thing is I had to sit there for ten minutes listening to that bar tenders lame jokes just to get this drink."

They both have a laugh before it dawns on Monica that Paris is actually out at the club alone. Never one to venture off to a nightclub by herself it makes Monica wonder what exactly is going on.

"So, what are you doing here?" Monica brazenly asks. Paris takes a moment to answer. She moves around toward the bar and finds a seat on one of the tall bar chairs. Leaning back against the bar she answers. "I was invited."

Monica gives her a cold stare before realizing just what she means. There could be only one person in the club that would interest Paris and give her cause to come out to the club alone by herself. "Navarro!" Monica blurts out.

Paris turns to her as if she has been found guilty of something or that her secret is out. "What do you mean?" Paris asks. Monica just stares at her. "Don't give me that." she says. "You know what I'm talking about."

Paris goes silent, as does Monica. With a look of jealousy on her face Monica focuses on the stage and the rest of the drink that's in her hand. Just as Paris is about to speak Navarro walks up. He greets them. "Hello ladies."

With his eyes fixed on Paris he barely notices Monica nonetheless his greeting was for the two of them. Monica gives him the cold shoulder while Paris shyly responds back. "Hi."

Navarro moves in closer to Paris and grabs her hand. At that moment she lifts her head and gives him a subtle smile but her eyes, locked with his, speak volumes.

"So, you came" he says. She just nods and smiles trying hard to keep her composure. Apparent she is still feeling the effects of their first encounter alone together.

"I'm glad you could make it." Navarro says. Paris tilts her head to the side with a smile she replies. "I wouldn't want to miss my world premiere."

Monica sits with a bewildered look on her face. Mind boggling how could this have happened she wonders. She tries hard to act like she is not paying attention all the while eavesdropping on the conversation, as she doesn't want to miss any juicy points.

As Papa D and The Crew finish their set the club announcers' voice is heard throughout the club calling for applause. The crowd roars with applause showing their adoration for Papa D and his group. The band gracefully walks off stage giving Navarro his cue that he must go on. He turns to Paris reaching out for her hand.

"I have to go now, I'm up next." he says.

Paris looks at him and smiles "Ok."

She gently releases his hand as he turns away and walks toward the stage. As if he forgot something he turns back and walks toward Paris. He leans in close to her and kisses her softly on her cheek. He whispers in her ear "Don't go anywhere. I will be right back."

Again, he turns and walks toward the stage. Monica then turns to Paris her eyes filled with envy. She blurts out "You slut!"

Shocked, all Paris can do is roll her eyes and look away. At that moment the lights go dim. The announcer in a low deep voice is the only thing heard.

"Ladies and gentlemen, Mr. Navarro Love."
The crowd applauds as soft blue light accents the stage. Navarro sits on a stool behind a microphone while the rest of the stage is covered in darkness. The only thing visible is his frame and the microphone stand. Paris watches intensely as Navarro swoons the audience. His voice flirts with different levels. A creamy tenor blends with a sexy falsetto. He stands behind his microphone moving his hands as if he were making love to it, caressing it with his fingers. His eyes survey the club until he finds Paris.

He delivers line after line, a song complimenting a man's admiration for his woman. In his song he asks. "What is the answer, to the question that is you? What shall I live for, what shall I do? Shall I build a cathedral for you? Layered in precious stones. Tell me what you wish for. Is it diamonds or gold?"

Her eyes find his as he moves across the stage. The light follows him as if it were his shadow, accenting his slim build. The song begins to climax as light fills the stage. Navarro points his finger toward Paris as his feelings are conveyed to her in song.

"You're the love, that I'm reaching for. It's drowning me I can't ignore. Inside your arms I wish to die, together. You're my priest to whom I confess my sins. And our love shall never end. Let us walk this road till the end of time together."

The words fill Paris' heart with untapped emotion. So many feelings she didn't know she had swell within her heart as tears begin to roll down her face.

The song comes to a close as the lights go down on stage. A roar of applause comes from the crowd. Paris spilling with emotion jumps from her seat and runs out of the club crying. Monica in a rush grabs her purse and runs after her. She finally catches up to her outside of the club.

"What's wrong with you?" She frantically asks. Uncontrollably Paris can't stop crying. She struggles to find the words to say.

Just repeating, "I can't, I can't."
Monica grabs her by the arm and tries to calm her down.

"You can't? What do you mean, what's wrong?" she asks again.

Paris wipes the tears from her eyes and takes a breath.

"Just tell him I had to go okay. I can't explain now" she says to Monica.

Monica sensing that something is deeply wrong acknowledges and nods her head. "Okay I will."

Paris turns and rushes off. Monica watches as Paris grows increasingly out of sight lost in the crowd of people on the street. She yells out to her, "Call me later." as Paris disappears out of sight.

Back inside the club Navarro walks off stage. After completing his performance, he makes his way back to the bar. He sees an empty bar stool noticing both Paris and Monica have left. He stands there for a moment looking for her.

He looks around the club as the many club members come by and congratulate him on a great performance. Though the one he wishes were there is nowhere to be found.

Disappointed he stands no longer. He walks away from the bar. He knows she has left, but why without saying a word. He wonders what he could have done to make her leave. With no answers his confusion quickly turns to anger as he feels Paris has snubbed him. In a flash the feeling he once held for Paris is challenged by his feelings of being discarded by her. Like the many memories of his past he locks his feelings away. The heart he once gave to Paris is now as cold as winter.

21

Nightmares Return

THE NIGHTMARES RETURN while Navarro sleeps. His mind is enveloped in total darkness. Only the sound of a child whimpering is heard. Suddenly a door bursts open, blinding light cuts through the darkness to reveal a 10 years old child. He sits cowering in the corner of a closet with tears falling from his eyes. Through the light a figure appears. Only the silhouette of their frame is noticeable, but he can make out that this figure hovering over him means to harm him. Navarro retreats quickly. He sinks deeper into the corner of the closet clutching his knees to his chest. The door slams shut, sending a loud crash echoing through the dark. Drowning out all hopes of light and salvation as the dark is all that's left.

Navarro awakes suddenly from his dream. He sits in bed as sweat drips from his forehead. His head begins to pound as the sound of the door slammed shut resonates through his mind. A terrible mind twisting pain causes him to lie back down. He wonders where it all comes from. He covers his eyes hoping that soon the pain will end.

All of a sudden, he hears singing. The unmistakable sound of his grandfather's voice comes from the kitchen. Always a blissful and calming sound it helps to ease his pounding headache. Soon after he notices the smell of breakfast in the air. Navarro gets up slowly to join his grandfather in the kitchen. He makes his way to the hallway taking light steps as to not aggravate his headache.

Walking down the hallway he reaches the kitchen door. He peeks around the corner and sees his grandfather standing there with his back to the doorway. Delray stands against the stove preparing breakfast. Humming a familiar tune his movements flow with the melody. Navarro comes in and sits at the table pulling a plate close to him. Delray at that moment turns and sees Navarro there.

"Good morning young blood. Just in time." he says.

Taking the food from stove he brings it over to the kitchen table. He fills Navarro's plate. The look of the food is totally uninviting, as Navarro can't help but to stare at this meal. Wondering if it will be his last as his grandfather is not the best cook.

Placing the skillet food back on the stove, Delray quickly takes his place at the table. Navarro sits silent staring at his plate. Although Delray knows Navarro isn't the best fan of his cooking, he notices that there is something more on his mind. After a brief moment of silence Delray reaches out to him.

"You want to tell me what's wrong?" he asks. After a moment Navarro snaps out of his silence. He grabs his fork and digs into his food. "I'm okay pop." he responds.

He drops his eyes and focus' on his plate. The distance has been growing between the two of them lately and it has become apparent to Delray that something has got to give. Not one to give up he digs deeper.

"Still having trouble sleeping?" The question catches Navarro off guard, he didn't know that his grandfather was aware of the nightmares. He thinks to himself for a moment "How could he possibly know?"

He becomes a little nervous and on edge. He shrugs his shoulders signaling he doesn't want to talk about it. He becomes even more focused on the meal in front of him.

"I know about the dreams son." Delray says to him.

Navarro doesn't look at him. Regressed he has nothing to say he just sits there silent. Delray tries again to reach out to him. "Do you want to talk about it?"

Navarro drops his eyes. He shakes his head answering "No." Delray moves his plate from in front of him and leans in closer to Navarro.

"Don't be afraid son. What's bothering you?" he pleads. Navarro lifts his head staring off into space. Pleading again Delray tries to breakthrough to him.

"We all have things that we have to deal with son. Don't run from it. Take hold of it. Beat it."

All of Navarro's emotions become apparent on his face. Feelings of anger, sadness, and fear build within him. His face turns red as his eyes begin to water.

Delray moves his chair closer to Navarro. He grabs his hand and lifts his head.

"Whatever you're going through I'm here with you." Navarro lowers his head unable to control the feelings within him he cannot hold back his tears any longer. His breathing becomes heavy as his tear's flow.

"Talk to me son." Delray begs. "Is it about your mother? I miss her too"

The question hits a chord in Navarro. His heavy breathing stops as if his heart has done the same. The tears have emptied. He lifts his head and wipes the remaining tears from his face. Delray leans into him as Navarro gets up from his chair.

Navarro places his hand on Delray's shoulder. He leans down to him and kisses him on the forehead. "I love you pop" he says. The only words he says as he leaves the kitchen.

Delray turns to Navarro just as he leaves the kitchen. "I know you do son. I know." He then turns back in his chair. He sits there alone and in silence. Wondering to himself, what can he do to help. He worries that if he cannot reach Navarro it may become worse. He is frustrated that he has no control. Things were a lot easier when Navarro was that 10years old child holding on to his grandfather for answers to all that was wrong in the world.

Delray grabs the plates from the table and places them on the counter. His mind swirls with thoughts of helplessness. The one thing he loves more than music he cannot fix. His frustration grows stronger as he slams the remaining dishes down on the counter. The glass shatters, jagged shards fly in all directions. Delray slams his fists on the counter in frustration releasing the tension within. "Damn it!" he yells.

His husky voice resonates throughout the kitchen. He looks down at the damage and takes a moment to gather his thoughts. He also takes that same moment to calm takes himself before picking up the many shattered pieces of glass.

With a bit of irony, he gives a slight yet sarcastic smile as the pieces of glass reminds him of the life and connection between Navarro and his mother. Once together now broken, he wishes putting them back together were just as easy.

As that togetherness in his opinion is the answer to all of Navarro's problems. The answer to comfort his pain and the substance that can fill the emptiness that has long been inside of him. But of course, doing so is impossible as no one has the power to bring Navarro's mother back to him.

For Delray he felt the years that have past healed many of those wounds. On this morning he feels helpless as he feels he has in some ways failed Navarro by taking the years of silence for granted instead of addressing the past that has now been allowed to resurface.

22

Starting Over

THE CLUB IS VIRTUALLY EMPTY only the daily clean up crew and a skeleton shift of workers are present. The sound of a piano comes from the dimly lit stage as Navarro sits trying to finish his composition.

His pain, passion, and heartache all come forth as he translates his feelings to paper. He works hard, breaking only to take a sip of water from a half empty glass sitting atop of the piano. It's becoming more difficult for him to focus as he is bothered by the affects of his frequent headaches. The pain becomes stronger as he plays so he stops for a moment to wait out another headache. He folds his arms on the piano and lays his head on them to rest. The silence is his sanctuary. He becomes lost within the quiet and the darkness. He closes his eyes falling deep into a meditative state.

Just as he becomes fully engulfed in his thoughts, he hears a voice.

"Penny for your thoughts." The voice sounds very familiar. He remembers his mother's voice and her comforting words whenever something was wrong with him.

But it could not be her voice. "Penny for your thoughts." There it is again. He raises his head to see a figure standing there in the dark. He squints his eyes to focus. "Could it be?" he thinks to himself. "No, I must be seeing things."

Suddenly his eyes bring into focus the figure standing before him. It's Paris. "What did you say?" he asks.

Paris walks closer to the stage. The stage lights from overhead accent the beautiful features of her face. "I said, penny for your thoughts. I don't know, it was something my mother used to say when I was upset about something."

Navarro's mind becomes clearer as he sits up from the piano. "What are you doing here?" he asks, seemingly uninterested in her explanation of her comments.

Making her way up the stairs onto the stage she says. "I'm sorry if I interrupted you. Your grandfather told me you might be here."

Navarro quickly gets up from the piano bench and walks toward the edge of the stage. "I see, so what do you want?" he says.

Of course, upset by the way she ran out on him during his show the other night. Paris senses the tension between the two, as to be expected.

"I wanted to talk about the other night." she explains.

Navarro feeling another headache coming on rubs his forehead.

"Don't worry about it." he says to her. He walks over to the piano and grabs the sheet music he was working on. After collecting his paperwork, he turns and walks toward the steps. Paris watches him turn his back to her. At a loss as to what to do next she just yells out to him.

"Please, talk to me. Just talk to me." Navarro stops before he reaches the steps. He turns to her. "What more could you have to say? You said enough when you left."

He stares at her for a moment. She has no response, lost are her words. She looks around the room searching for the words to say. Navarro grows tired of standing there so he begins to walk down the steps. Frustrated Paris stands there about to burst with emotion. She struggles to find any words to say. Before Navarro reaches the last step, she yells out to him. "I love you!"

She yells so loud that everyone in the club stops what they were doing. Navarro stops, frozen he does not move.

"I'm in love with you Navarro." she says as he stands with his back to her. He turns to her. Silently staring somewhat in shock. Paris flushed with emotion frantically tries to explain her actions.

"I was scared, ok. I just didn't know what was happening." she says as her voice begins to shutter.

Navarro makes his way back up the steps toward her as she begins to cry uncontrollably. Her words run together flustered, as all of her emotions have taken control of her. She pleads to him. "I just had to get away, I'm sorry. I'm sorry."

He reaches her and quickly wraps his arms around her. "Shhh, its ok." he tries to calm her. He wipes the tears from her face, the more he wipes the more they run down her cheeks. "I love you." she says. "I have loved you since the first day I saw you. I just didn't know how to handle it or what to do or say."

Navarro takes her in his arms. He holds her tightly next to his chest. He whispers to her. "I love you too." He then places both of his hands on her face bringing her lips closer to his. He gently kisses her. Her crying stops as all of her passion and frustrations are released in her kiss. The kiss lasts for what seems like hours as the sweet, yet bitter mix of tears mingles between their lips. Locked within each other's arms Navarro pulls back to look at her.

"Do you want to get out of here?" he asks. She doesn't say a word she just nods her head to signal and defiant yes. The two of them make their way to the edge of the stage. Navarro quickly moves in front. He grabs Paris' hand and leads her down the steps. The two of them quickly make their way to the front of the club disappearing in the shadows toward the exit.

Navarro throws the door open as they exit. The huge glass doors slowly close behind them. Leaving behind their false impressions and bent emotions they make their way to their next destination, the start of a new beginning.

23

The Lake

COOL WINTER WINDS blow across the surface of massive Lake Michigan. Seagulls fly and the harmonic sound of birds singing whistles through the air. Navarro and Paris stand holding one another against the railing of the boardwalk. They look out and admire the beauty of Lake Michigan in late winter while sharing the warmth of one another. Leaning against the railing they look out over the water.

"This is so beautiful. I could stay here all day." Paris says. Leaning a little more to look over the edge of the boardwalk. Navarro moves in closer to Paris. Standing behind her he wraps his arms around her waist pulling her closer to him. She smiles then leans back against his chest. They gaze out at the water watching the bird's fly low dipping into the water before quickly taking off back into the air.

The wind picks up bringing a chilling cold across the water. "It's so cold out here." Paris says. Cuddling closer to Navarro. "But that's why I have you here."

Navarro leans in closer to her and kisses her cheek. It's so cold that he barely feels his lips press against Paris' rose-colored cheek. After the kiss he takes a moment to breathe in the crisp cool air. Taking note of Paris' scent and the jasmine scented perfume she's wearing.

"It is beautiful." he says, admiring the horizon as well as Paris' profile.
"Kind of amazing really"

Paris turns her head slightly to face him. "Amazing?' she asks.

Navarro placing his lips close to her ear responds softly.

"Something so beautiful can be in front of so many people yet simply go unnoticed."

With every word Paris draws closer to Navarro. The affect of his voice soft yet filled with passion and substance makes it hard for her to resist any word that he speaks.

She looks out over the water before becoming intrigued about the man whose arms she finds so comforting.

"So, Mr. Love, what's your story?" she asks playfully. Navarro looks a little shocked by the question he can only ask one of his own.

"My story? What do you mean?" Paris turns to him making sure his arms do not let her go. Facing him staring in his eyes she asks again. "Yes, your story? You never answered my question the other night."

Navarro shyly looks away, a little taken back as he doesn't know exactly where this conversation is going, nor does he know exactly what Paris is searching for. Cautiously he asks. "What question did you ask?"

Paris takes a moment to scan her words carefully.

"You just seem so different. The music, the writing, where does it all come from?" she asks.

She stares searching for the answer in his eyes. Trying to read his emotions and feelings she finds it hard to make out exactly why he is holding back. She patiently waits for an answer. Pleading with him she presses for him to give her something.

"Tell me." she says. Navarro turns his head and responds. "Well its kind of complicated."

Paris touches him gently on the chin and moves his face in her direction to connect with his eyes.

"I don't care, tell me" she says softly. Looking deeper within his eyes she tries to remove the barrier between them. In her gaze she lets him know that she is not going anywhere until her question is answered.

After a moment of contemplating just exactly what he should do it happens, Navarro gives in.

"Well I began playing when I was about ten." he explains. "I'm not sure where it came from really. I mean my grandfather taught me, but it came rather natural to me."

Paris finding an opening asks more. "What about your mom, where is she?"

Struck by what she asks Navarro quickly pulls away. Noticeably avoiding the question. Paris, feeling she has overstepped her bounds quickly apologizes. "I'm sorry I didn't mean to be rude."

Navarro motions to her with a wave of his hand that he is okay. He walks over to the other side of the boardwalk and leans over the railing. With his back to her he continues to open up.

"Its okay. My mother died a long time ago" he says. Paris feels her heart sink within her chest.

"Oh my God I'm sorry to hear that." she says. Placing her hand over her mouth somewhat feeling the extension of his pain. She walks up slowly behind him and placing one hand on his back rubbing it gently. "It's okay." he says. "It was a long time ago."

At a loss for words Paris continues to rub his back. She stands behind him waiting for an opening hoping she won't create another awkward mood with her questions. Changing the mood Navarro quickly shifts subjects.

"So, what about you?" he asks. Paris feeling as if she has been let off the hook jumps at the question. "Me?" she says.

Navarro turns to her with his stare he focus' intently on her eyes. "Yes, you. Where did you learn to dance?" he asks.

Paris smiles uncontrollably before giving the backdrop as to how she fell in love with dancing. "I've always loved to dance." she says. "Ever since I was a little girl, I would beg my mother to take me for lessons."

She walks to his side and leans her back against the guardrail. " I've always wanted to be one of those girls you would see on television or on Broad Way just dancing, I Love it." she says enthusiastically.

She leaps from the railing to stand behind him. She wraps her arms around him and lays her head against his back.

"What do you love, besides music?" she asks. Navarro takes a second to scan his thoughts. He turns to her and wraps his arms around her. Looking in her eyes he says softly. "I love you."

Only the sun shines brighter than the smile on her face. She moves in closer to him to kiss him deeply on the lips. With each kiss they fall deeper for one another.

Losing awareness of their surroundings, the birds become quiet the wind becomes still. For a moment it feels as if they are the only two on the boardwalk, possibly the only two in the world. Bringing their kiss to a close Paris opens her eyes to see Navarro staring back at her.

"You want to get out of here?" she asks. Navarro taken back by the question asks. "Where do you want to go?" Paris kisses him gently on the lips before responding.

"I will choose this time. Do you want to go?" Although wondering just what she has in mind, Navarro nods his head in confirmation that he wants to follow.

"Come with me." Paris says with a smile. They walk off together with Paris leading the way to a destination to which this time, only she knows where it will end.

24

Paris' Love

THE DOOR OPENS to a small studio apartment. Suddenly Paris walks in followed by Navarro. "Wait here." she says. "Make yourself comfortable."

Navarro stands in the center of the living room surveying the surroundings. A dancer's utopia, her apartment parallels his home. The walls littered with posters of former dancers and posters from stage plays. Ballet shoes hang from the walls. He walks to her mantle and takes notice of the many pictures from her childhood, pictures documenting her growth as a woman and as a dancer.

For a moment he stands there envious of her childhood. From the smile adorning her face on every picture seems it was without strife or hardship, totally contradictory to his childhood. As he investigates further, he hears a voice from behind him.

"Navarro." Speaking in a soft sensual tone Paris stands behind him with her back against the wall. He turns quickly noticing the red satin robe covering her slim frame.

"Come here, I want to show you something" she says. Navarro wastes no time moving closer to her. He moves quickly yet taking measured steps as to not show that he is too anxious for what's to come next.

He looks her up and down admiring her shape her long smooth legs show from the short cut robe. He reaches her as they immediately begin to kiss. Their excitement and passion unleashed as they throw themselves into one another's emotions.

Their kissing leads them down the hallway toward Paris' room. They move against the walls caressing and kissing one another softly, but with much determination.

He picks her up and holds her against the wall as her legs wrap around his waist. His lips move from her neck to her chest slowly tasting every inch of her body. They reach Paris' bedroom and the scent of lavender fills the air. The room is decorated with a sea of candles.

The light and warmth of the candles engulf the room as Navarro lays Paris down on the bed and massages her body with his tongue. He moves from the back of her neck to the small of her back, her body trembles as he caresses her beautiful frame.

She turns to him and quickly throws him to the bed. Straddling him she holds his arms against the bed while kissing his neck and moving her lips to his chest. The two of them reveal to one another the extent of their love as they create a love unparalleled.

Drifting deeper into the abyss of love that has captured the two of them they melt unto one another. Seconds turn to minutes and minutes to hours as they share one another's passion and affections. The only sound heard is the sound of their breathing as their lovemaking becomes more intense. Thrusting their bodies at one another they begin to climax.

Together they begin to peak and with one powerful collision as if two cars hit head on, they come together. Paris falls on top of Navarro breathing heavy and drenched with sweat. Her breathing mirrored by his they both bask in the aftermath of their shared experience. As Paris lays on top of Navarro he cradles her in his arms. He wraps them tightly around her so tight their bodies remain as one.

They lay lifeless not speaking, not saying a word. Their breathing becomes in sync. Fast quick breaths gradually become slower and longer. As time passes the light of the candles grow dimmer the flame not as high. The light fades and the two of them fall asleep locked within each other's arms. What was once engulfed in light now the room is still, silent and in darkness.

As the night grows long the two of them are lost within their dreams. Paris finding herself sleeping peacefully, yet Navarro lies asleep being haunted once again by his nightmares return. He dreams of walking into his home standing in the center of the living room witnessing the chaos again, furniture overturned, glass broken, and his mother lying in the corner.

He walks over to her hoping that the outcome will be different this time. He kneels down to her turning her over to look at her face. Her body lies lifeless.

"I'm sorry momma, I'm sorry." he says as he bends over to kiss her forehead. Suddenly her eyes open staring directly at him. Navarro jumps and awakes from his dream trembling and screaming out for his mother. His head begins to pound as the headaches begin again. The pain is unbearable as he grabs his head with both hands closing his eyes tightly shut.

Paris awakes from her sleep to find Navarro sweating and in pain next to her. She quickly reaches out to him putting her arm around his back.

"What's wrong baby?" she asks confused and concerned. Navarro doesn't answer he sits holding his head rocking back and forth in the bed trying to endure the pain. The dreams and the pain of his headaches overwhelm him as his emotions take hold. Pleading with him Paris becomes upset.

"Please tell me what's wrong." She begs of him. Paris, seeing that Navarro is crying, can't contain her emotions. Her eyes swell with tears as she grabs him and hugs him begging for an answer. Frantically she scrambles to help him.

"Should I call somebody?" she asks with her voice shaking in fear.

"No!" Navarro says. "I'm okay." At a loss as to what to do she can only sit there next to him crying.

"I don't know what to do. Please tell me what to do." she pleads. Navarro tries to calm himself in order to calm Paris. He takes a second to get his thoughts and emotions under control. First, he controls his breathing then wipes his tears.

"I'm okay now." he says to Paris trying to comfort her. Seeing that he is okay she then gathers her emotions. Still upset she pleads for him to open up to her.

"Please tell me what's going on" she says. Moving closer to him in bed rubbing his back. Navarro sits silent before laying his head on Paris' lap.

"I keep seeing her." he says. "I keep seeing her face." Paris rubs his head trying to comfort him. "Seeing who?" she asks.

Navarro closes his eyes and takes in the comforting touch of Paris rubbing his head. Her touch eases his headache and allows him open up to her.

"My mother." he says. "I keep seeing my mother." Paris stops for a moment not knowing exactly what to do or say she asks him to continue.

"Please tell me what happened." she says as she begins to rub his neck and back again. Very solemn he replies. "She was killed."

Paris stops rubbing his back and places her hand over her mouth in shock. His tears begin again as he recalls what happened.

"They said she was beaten to death." he says with his voice cracking.

"I was too young to do anything. I couldn't help her." Seeing the hurt and pain in his face Paris can no longer contain and or control her emotions, she begins to cry with him.

"I'm so sorry baby" she says to him. She takes her hand and gently wipes the tears from his face. He continues to explain the basis of his pain and the past that haunts him.

"I keep seeing it over and over. I'm just standing there I can't move. I try but I just can't." The pain of his headache lingers this time seeming it will never end. Navarro sits up in the bed wiping his tears and holding his head. Paris sits behind him on her knees and wraps her arms around him. She lays her head on his shoulder and squeezes him tightly. With his hands covering his face he tries to shake his headache and his painful memories. " I miss her so much." he says. "I miss her everyday."

Navarro leans back resting his head against Paris chest. She comforts him the only way she knows how, with words "Its okay baby" she says, holding back her tears while trying to be strong for the both of them.

Navarro tries to relax as Paris tries to take his pain away with her comforting touch. The two of them sit cradling one another. As Paris rubs his head their interaction has transformed yet again. She now takes on the role of not only his lover but also his comforter gently easing the pain within him. Although these are uncharted waters, she is more than willing to assume the role. She wants nothing more than to help Navarro heal no matter how tough the task. In order to assist she will do what she must to help him over come this pain he holds deep within.

25

A Strong Voice

MORNING BRINGS CALM. Navarro walks into the kitchen to the sound of his grandfather singing and making breakfast. As he walks in Delray is surprised but happy to see him.

"Good morning young blood. Didn't expect to see you this morning" he says. The smile on his face accents the years of wrinkles brought on by stress and old age. He takes his breakfast over to the kitchen table and takes a seat.

"I wanted to come see you before I went to rehearsal." Navarro says watching his grandfather take a seat. Sliding a chair out from under the table Delray motions for Navarro to sit down.

"I see, well come have a seat. Have some breakfast."

Reluctantly Navarro walks over to the table. "I can't really pop. I just came to see you before I headed to rehearsal."

Delray again motions for Navarro to sit down. Knowing he is fighting a losing battle Navarro pulls the chair away from the table and plops down.

Delray pauses for a moment then slides his plate of food closer to him. He takes a bite of his breakfast taking a few seconds to chew before swallowing. Navarro just sits wondering exactly what it is his grandfather wants to discuss since neither of them has said a word. Delray takes another bite before placing his fork in his plate. Wiping his mouth with the napkin on his lap he gingerly removes the crumbs of food before speaking. With a low husky tone, he says.

"Is there something you want to talk to me about?" Looking Navarro directly in his eyes. Navarro stares back avoiding the question. Delray looks him defiantly in the eye almost as if he is looking through him. He says to him.

"Son whatever is inside of you taking hold of you like this, you can beat it." Navarro disconnects lowering his head. Giving up he quickly says. "Okay pop."

As he tries to get up from the table Delray grabs his wrist. Instructing Navarro to sit back down he guides him to his chair. "Son please, sit back down."

He continues to try to connect with Navarro offering his guidance just as a coach tries to coach their team.

"These past few years I've witnessed something wonderful. I've seen you grow from a young boy to a man," he says moving his chair closer to Navarro. Placing his hand on Navarro's shoulder, his strength and guidance is felt in his touch.

"I am so proud of you," he says. "If your mother was here, she would say the same."

Navarro pulls back as if he doesn't want to hear anymore. Delray places his other hand on Navarro's shoulder. Delray makes eye contact and says to him. "She is with you son, always. Remember that I am with you as well."

Navarro gives a quick nod to show he understands but says nothing. After a second of silence Delray releases his shoulders. 'I love you" he says to Navarro. Getting up from the table Navarro responds back. "I love you too pop."

He tries to walk out of the kitchen, but Delray jumps from his chair and quickly wraps his arms around Navarro to hug him. The embrace so strong nearly blocks the wind from entering Navarro's lungs. Nonetheless he wraps his arms around his grandfather returning the hug with the same intensity. After their embrace Navarro heads toward the living room. Before leaving his grandfather calls out to him with a bit of levity.

"You sure you don't want breakfast?" he asks. Waiting for a response he sits back down at the table and brings his plate close to him. All he hears next is the front door closing shut. He doesn't take a bite of food he just lowers his head and brings his hands closer to his face. He closes his eyes and begins to pray. This prayer is one not for himself. He is praying for an answer, he is praying for Navarro.

26

Whispering Silence

THE ORCHESTRA BEGINS rehearsing the closing piece Navarro has prepared for his upcoming performance. The conductor Mr. Perry gathers everyone in place for another run through. As Navarro takes his place behind a large grand piano, Paris takes a seat in the audience to watch.

"Okay let's begin again." Mr. Perry instructs. He turns to Navarro and with a raised eyebrow he asks. "Are you ready Mr. Navarro?"

Navarro takes a breath and nods his head to signal that he is ready. Raising his hands to draw everyone's attention Mr. Perry says softly. "Okay let's begin."

After a moment of silence, they begin. As the string section brings the introduction of the piano, Navarro intensely focused places his hands on the piano keys. Back at home Delray sits in his study focused on finishing a composition of his own. He sits down at his piano and places his hands on the keys.

As if the two are in sync Navarro and Delray take the same posture. Their fingers align within the same key. The strings bring in Navarro as the conductor motions for him to begin. Navarro methodically runs through the scales of music effortlessly.

Delray begins to play as their music seemingly becomes intertwined. Their play is fluid. Suddenly with a burst of emotion Navarro vigorously goes into his piece, the intensity visible on his face as he plays with his eyes closed. Delray's hands begin flow faster moving up and down the keys. Keeping pace with each stroke.

The two of them strike a chord their passion and expression mirrored by one another. The piece moves faster and faster like the pounding of a heartbeat. Navarro becomes more and more aggressive as he plays so much so that unbeknownst to him his nose begins to bleed.

Harder and harder he wills his fingers to do what his mind wants. Delray displays intensity and emotion aged and skilled. Navarro pounds the keys ringing out a melody hard yet sweet. It moves faster and harder than suddenly with a burst and flare it ends.

Navarro pauses as if his heart has just stopped. He leans his head forward and notices the blood trickling from his nose. The blood streams from his nose making it impossible for him to stop it with just his hands and fingers. He covers his face as Mr. Perry and members of the orchestra notice. He jumps from behind the piano and bolts toward the exit.

"Sorry I have to go" he says with his mouth muffled. As he runs off stage Mr. Perry tries to stop and assist him. Alarmed and concerned he says.

"Oh my God, are you okay?" Navarro doesn't answer he just runs toward the exit dripping blood in his wake. Paris watches and becomes worried recalling Navarro's episode from the night before. Running toward the auditorium exit she catches him in the hallway. Screaming "Navarro wait!" as she runs after him.

Leaving everyone in the auditorium wondering what has just happened the only thing they can do is sit in amazement. Back at Navarro's home there is silence. Delray has stopped playing as well. The house sits still very quiet. Suddenly the quiet is interrupting with a loud bang as the front the door bursts open. Running through the door is Navarro screaming out for his grandfather. "Pop, pop!" He yells but receives no answer. He hears nothing. It's silent. Very unusual to Navarro as he quickly takes notice.

The usual singing or whistling has been replaced by eerie silence. Navarro walks through the house slowly. He walks past the kitchen and notices a cup of tea sitting on the table. He makes his way to the study. Navarro begins to enter the study but is stopped by a sudden blow to his chest. He's frozen. He tries to move but he can't. In an instant his eyes are fixed on something. His heart sinks as he musters the strength to walk further in the study. He reaches the piano and there on the floor his grandfather lies lifeless.

The image so vivid it brings his past to reality once more. Navarro walks over to his grandfather's body and kneels down beside him. He places his hand on his grandfather's forehead and leans over to kiss him. His feelings and emotions erupt inside of him, as he breaks down crying cradled over his grandfather's body.

Paris following him to the house finally walks through the door. Upon entering she calls him from the living room. "Navarro, where are you?" she calls.

She walks down the hallway hearing what sounds like Navarro. She follows the sound of his crying. She reaches the study and is immediately floored by what she sees. She drops to her knees and places her hand over her mouth. "Oh my God baby, I'm sorry."

Navarro doesn't respond he just lies there hovering over his grandfather weeping uncontrollably. His crying triggers Paris' emotions as she begins to cry with him and for him. She keeps her distance not moving too close to him. She doesn't want to pull him away for she knows it would be impossible.

She just sits and watches Navarro unravel. The pain is too much. All at once his emotions burst out of him. Screaming at the top of his lungs he yells out to his mother calling her name. For what seems like an eternity his screams last forever. With all the strength drained out of him he gives one last yell before collapsing on top of his grandfather. He lays frozen clutching Delray's body. He can neither scream nor fight any longer. His body gives up as he falls limp.

27

The Funeral

THE MORNING IS COLD AND CLOUDY. An overcast day, as the heavy clouds try hard to hold back the rain. Friends and family of Delray "Papa D" have come to pay their respects to him as he is laid to rest. Navarro sits stoic as his pain has come full circle. Paris next to him holds his hand as Delray's casket is lowered into the ground.

While the casket is being lowered the images return. Navarro has flashbacks of his mother's funeral. Flashing through his mind they begin to give him pulsating headache. He rubs the bridge of his nose to ease the pain. Paris notices he is in pain and places her arm around him to console him.

After the preacher takes a moment to say the last words Paris leans over to Navarro and whispers in his ear. "Are you going to be okay?" she asks. Navarro nods his head not saying a word, but signaling yes.

Paris pulls him closer and whispers again. "Do you want to go?" Navarro lowers his head still thriving in pain he takes a moment to respond. "Yes, let's go" he says.

Navarro and Paris get up from their seats. As they leave everyone watches and says their last respects to Delray. As everyone gets an opportunity to lay a rose on the casket the rain begins to fall. Navarro and Paris reach her car, she sits him down in the passenger seat before running around to her side jumping in the car quickly to avoid the rain.

Navarro leans his seat back and lays his head against the headrest. Paris doesn't know what to say she just starts the car and slowly pulls off. Navarro turns his head to look out the window taking one last look at where he leaves his grandfather. Heartbroken that he will never see him again. So many things mirror his past. How can one deal with so much alone? How can one individual have such bad luck?

The ride is long. The sound of the rain beating against the car nearly drowns out the sound of Charlie Parker's Ugly Beautiful playing on the radio. Navarro closes his eyes and remembers the ride he took to his grandfathers' house after leaving his mothers' burial. The vision is all too real. His life seems to be an endless circle of pain to which he knows not why it happens to him. He wonders to himself why. Why a life has to be filled with such strife.

He asks, but he can't answer that question. Often, he tries, but he cannot answer. He deals and moves on pushing aside the pain, pushing aside his feelings. His mind goes blank. He doesn't want to think of anything anymore. He doesn't want to remember the past or deal with the present. In darkness there is silence. He finds solace there. Unbeknownst to him his sanctuary of darkness is also his prison. Not one of a physical nature but mental his mind is the source of his imprisonment.

Finally, the ride comes to an end. Paris pulls the car to the curb outside of Navarro's house. The silence is awkward but understandable to her that Navarro isn't speaking much. As the car stops, she reaches over to grab his hand. "Here we are." she says softly.

Navarro sits up in his seat and peers out the window at his house. A little hesitant he doesn't open the car door he just sits for a moment.

Paris asks. "Do you want me to come in?" Hoping that he will accept her offer. Navarro nonetheless rejects.

"No, you go ahead. I'm okay." he assures her. Paris squeezing his hand with a little pressure trying to reach him asks again. "Are you sure?"

Navarro takes a second before responding. "Yes, I'm okay. I just want to be alone."

Paris doesn't pressure him any further she releases his hand as he opens the car door.

"Wait." she says. Navarro turns to her. "Will you call me later?" she asks. Navarro nods his head, the pain visible in his face. Paris reaches out to touch him again this time she grabs him and hugs him tightly around the neck. Navarro buries his face in her neck and hugs her back though his grasp is not as tight as hers. After a moment he pulls away. Paris gives him a soft kiss on his forehead and lets him go.

Navarro places one foot out of the door but is stopped by Paris again saying. "I love you." He pauses for a brief moment before turning to her. With slight eye contact he responds back. "I love you too."

This time the words are with less emotion, they are less connected. He gets out of the car and walks the long sidewalk leading to the front door. Paris is visibly shaken as she watches Navarro leave her. Not knowing what exactly is going through his mind, she worries but gives him the space he needs. She stays for a moment but the emotion inside of her builds. Frustrated as to what she can do she drives away in tears.

Navarro reaches the front door and walks in closing the door behind him. The silence is unnerving, as his home is empty. Void of his grandfathers singing his home has taken on a desolate tone. It doesn't feel like home anymore.

He goes through each room reminiscing on the day he first walked in with his grandfather. The feeling of being alone and on his own has come back to him. Building inside of him is his fear and anger that once enveloped his soul as a child. He walks to the wall framed with pictures of all the past great musicians. He notices a photo of his grandfather Delray, and The Crew. Becoming overwhelmed with emotion he slams his fist against the wall.

Suddenly his anger and fear grabs hold of him and he releases it with rage, pounding both fists against the wall. He turns his anger toward the pictures hanging there. He begins breaking the frames of the photos destroying them one by one slamming them to the floor. He then turns and bolts down the hallway. He moves from room to room destroying everything in his path till he makes his way to the study.

He knocks over chairs and lamps. Engulfed in his anger he destroys everything he can put his hands on. Unaware of the extent of his rage he turns over his grandfather's piano. In that moment he suddenly stops. The piano that his grandfather loved so much lay face down broken on one side next to dozens of papers.

All of his grandfather's sheet music lies strewn across the floor. Navarro falls to his knees crying. Picking up the papers he notices it's the same composition his grandfather was working on before he died. He takes a moment to focus clearing his eyes of his tears the best he can. Lost and alone he closes his eyes leaning against the piano hoping that once he opens them the pain would go away.

His heart beats strongly against his chest at a pace he has never felt. The pain, the struggles all have beaten him. He endures no more. He has given up. He falls completely to the floor and feels the cold hardwood against his back. The sheet music and broken pieces of furniture and glass surrounds him. He stares up at the ceiling with a frozen look on his face. He tries to scream but he can't. He tries to yell out to his grandfather, but no words come out just air, just his breath.

He reaches his arms out and grabs a bunch of the paper surrounding him. He cradles it in his arms and holds it tightly against his chest. He closes his eyes as the last few tears stream down his face. A part of him wishing he were to die his breathing becomes slower. His soul being outside of his body watches over him witnessing his own pain and demise. There lying on the floor is a man beaten. No optimism, the worst part of life has won. He lies in silence. He lies in rest.

28

The Storm

HOURS GO BY THE NIGHT IS SILENT. The only sound heard is that of raindrops falling from the sky finding their way to the ground with a continuous crash. Navarro's house is wrecked. Furniture turned on its side, pictures in broken frames, glass everywhere. It looks as if a tornado ran through and the only visible sign is the devastation left in its wake. The house is quiet, cold, and dark. Then suddenly through the darkness the silence is interrupted by a knock at the door. With no answer the knocking continues.

After several attempts the door opens and Paris appears. She walks in slowly calling to Navarro as she enters. "Navarro,

Navarro. Are you here?" she says, calling to him as she peers into the living room.

She opens the door wider and takes notice of the damage that has been done to the living room. She moves slowly becoming more worried considering Navarro is nowhere to be seen and he hasn't answered her call.

She moves from the living room making her way toward the back of the house. Stepping over the broken glass and picture frames she looks down and notices a photo of Navarro as a child with his mother. She picks up the photo and dusts off the pieces of glass littered across it. She pauses for a moment trying to understand why Navarro has done this before quickly moving forward in her search for him. She continues to call to him, yet still her calls go unanswered.

Paris walks the long cold hallway leading to the study. She moves closer to the doorway and as she enters, she sees Navarro lying on the floor curled in a ball lifeless. Her worries become greater as she rushes over to him. She kneels down on the floor and hovers over him. She takes both hands and tries to wake him.

"Navarro, baby get up." she screams frantically. Her worries are eased as he slowly rolls over. Still frantic she tries to wake him. Pleading with him she rocks him back and forth.

"Navarro it's me Paris, please baby, get up. Come on." Navarro slowly opens his eyes. Still groggy he speaks to her. "Leave me alone" he says pulling away from her.

Paris lets him go and sits down on her knees. "I was worried I didn't hear from you, so I came" she says with tears in her eyes.

Navarro turns his back to her and curls up shutting her out. Very cold he says, "I'm fine just go away."

Her feelings are crushed to hear Navarro speak to her this way. She begins to cry as each time she tries to touch him Navarro pushes her away and rolls over turning his back to her. She takes a second to gather herself before becoming defiant.

"No, I won't leave you like this" she says to him. Navarro becomes irate screaming at her "Don't you get it? I don't want you here. Leave me alone" he yells.

Paris' heart sinks. She sits there shocked and amazed. She has not seen this side of Navarro. He turns to her with all of his anger and frustration he takes it out on her.

"I don't need anybody" he says. Trying hard to hold back her tears Paris responds. "That's not true Navarro."

Still stern and unapologetic Navarro continues with each word he crushes her a little more. "I can manage on my own I've done it before."

Wiping the tears from her face Paris compassionately tells him. "You don't have to be alone."

Immediately Navarro corrects her. "I am alone" he say's "I have nothing now."

Paris tries her best to console him. "That's not true." she say's again. Navarro screams at her. "What do I have? Tell me. What do I have?"

Fuming and turning red his hurt and pain is visibly destroying him. Paris pauses for a moment to compose herself. Navarro stares at her waiting for an answer. She searches her thoughts as well as his eyes looking for a pathway into his heart again.

"You still have your music." she tells him.

"I'm sure your grandfather would've wanted you to keep doing that."

Her words only infuriate him further. He jumps from the floor throwing the papers he was holding to the ground. Pointing his finger in her face he yells at her.

"Don't talk to me about my grandfather. Just stop!" He paces back and forth as Paris sits on the floor watching. His emotions give way to tears. Not having the strength to stand any longer he falls to the floor on his knees. Paris quickly rushes to him and pulls him closer to her. He can't contain his feelings, so he releases them weeping in her arms. She squeezes him tight and speaks softly to him. "I know he loved you" she says. Navarro sobbing responds back. "I just can't do it anymore."

Paris begins rocking him in her arms as his pain is felt within her she begins to cry with him. "What do you mean?" she asks.

He tries to speak as his words are broken into pieces by his crying.

"How can I continue when everything I've ever known has left me? Everything I've cared for, everything I've loved has left me. I have nothing now."

He holds tight to Paris as she takes her hand and wipes his tears.

"Not everything has gone away." she say's. "I'm still here." Navarro looks up at her and takes solace in knowing that Paris genuinely cares for him. He looks in her eyes and sees the unconditional quality his mother once held for him. Paris stares back.

"I love you baby." she says. Pulling him closer. "I'm not going anywhere." She leans over and kisses his forehead. Navarro's tears are seemingly washed away by the love Paris has for him. He rests his head on her chest as she cradles him in her arms. He becomes very quiet, very still.

"They didn't leave you baby." she says to him. "They are still with you. Never forget them and they will always be here." she explains. "You have to learn to love them but let them go."

"I am afraid to." Navarro says. "If I let go, I will never have them again." Paris places her hand on Navarro's cheek. She kisses his lips then offers more words of comfort.

"In letting go you don't have to forget them baby. They will always be with you." she says. "And so, will I."

Navarro takes in everything she says. "It's just hard. It's so hard." he say's. Paris pulls him even closer so that he can feel her heart beat next to his.

"I know baby. I know it is." she says stroking his head as he rests in her arms. The two become closer than they have ever been. A bond between their hearts has been strengthened with their tears.

"I love you Paris." Navarro whispers to her. With a defiant whisper Paris responds back. "I love you too." She looks down at him witnessing the pain and burden he must shoulder alone. Navarro lies cradled in her arms. She slowly leans over to kiss him. They kiss, holding on to one another as if it were the last time they will ever see each other. As their kiss ends Paris pulls Navarro even closer to her chest. He rests his head against her chest as she lays her head to rest atop of his. The strength of their love is personified and cemented with their embrace.

29

A Dream Fulfilled

ONE MONTH LATER AND THE PERFORMANCE
DAY ARRIVES. Navarro sits in his dressing room alone staring
into the mirror. He then takes a photo of himself and his
grandfather and places it on the mirror. Suddenly the dressing
room door opens. Paris comes in with a small gift in her hands.
"Hey baby." she greets him.

Navarro sits with a smile on his face. "Hey." responding
back. "What are you doing back here?" he asks her.

Playfully she asks. "Do you want me to leave?" He quickly
answers. "No, no. I'm glad you're here."

Paris pulls up a chair to sit next to him. She reaches over to
grab his hand. "Today's a big day. Are you nervous?" she asks.

Navarro shrugs his shoulders as if he has become jaded by the numerous performances he has had over the years.

"How are you feeling?" Paris inquires.

Navarro takes a second before responding. He looks at the photo of himself and his grandfather attached to the mirror. He smiles then says. "I'm doing fine."

Hearing this brings a huge smile to Paris' face. "That's great baby" she says.

"I have a surprise for you." Anxious she places the gift in his hands.

"Open it." She says.
Navarro looks down at the small box and then back at her. "What is it?" he asks.

She tilts her head and with a huge smile instructs him to open the gift. Navarro slowly unwraps the gift to reveal a beautiful gold frame. Within the frame is a picture of him and his mother from years past, from his childhood. He looks at the picture then at Paris. She looks back at him waiting for his approval.

"Do you like it?" she asks. Navarro leans over to her and kisses her deeply on the lips. "Thank you, baby." he says before placing the picture next to the mirror. "You're welcome." Paris says. "Now get out of here and have a great show."

Navarro grabs Paris by the hand as they both stand up. He wraps his arms around her squeezing her tightly. "Thank you for everything." he whispers in her ear. Paris smiles and wipes the lipstick she left from his lips.

"Have a good show okay" she says walking out of the dressing room. Navarro walks toward the door. Before leaving he turns back to look at the photos on the desk. He blows a kiss goodbye to this mother and grandfather. He then turns out the light and walks out of the dressing room closing the door behind him.

The time has now come, thousands have gathered to witness the phenomenon that is Navarro and his music. No seat is left empty as the Orchestra warms for the performance. After a brief build up suddenly the lights go dim. Out walks the conductor Mr. Perry who takes his place atop the center podium. Offstage Navarro waits nervously with Paris by his side. He stands piercing out into the crowd from behind the curtain. Navarro takes Paris' hand. He brings her closer to him and kisses her gently on the lips one last time for good luck.

Mr. Perry cues for Navarro to walk out onto the stage. As he leaves Paris grabs his arm bringing him to her. She kisses him soft yet deep against his lips. After a moment she lets him go. Before he pulls away, she says to him with a smile.

"Good luck, I love you."

Navarro doesn't say a word. He just looks back at her and smiles before rushing out to a roaring applause. He takes his place behind a newly polished black grand piano. He looks at Mr. Perry before placing his hands on the keys. Once he is set Mr. Perry directs the Orchestra into an opening piece.

Slowly the auditorium goes completely dark. A spotlight dawns over Navarro and his piano. He begins to play a melody, sweet yet strong, fluid yet abrupt in movement. A melancholy mood resonates from the piano, changing somewhat between a feeling of love lost and love anew. The pace quickens and becomes stronger with each stroke of the keys. Bouncing high and low a sweet seduction of sound is generated. The pace grows quicker as the sound of violins and oboes pick up a deep pounding tone like thunder.

With a crash the lights come up and Navarro begins a ferocious solo faster and faster he strikes the piano as the orchestra keeps pace with him. Harder and faster he brings the piece to a heightened level of emotion not even he thought possible.

Vigorously he wavers in and out of the melody, the sound blissful and astonishing. Racing across the keys he brings his piece to a close, his hands moving faster and faster his emotion seeping onto his fingertips as he plays. As he plays his head begins to pound, the harder he plays the harder his head pounds and with a flash just as it begun the piece is over. Navarro stops for a moment there is silence. The crowd amazed begins to cheer and applaud. Navarro sits behind the piano with his head pounding and entranced, unaware of the applause from the crowd.

Mr. Perry calls to him to begin again. Navarro takes a moment to gather himself as Paris watches from the wing off stage. With a tear in her eye she begins to smile. The conductor waves his hands and the music begins again. The audience sits in full enjoyment at what their eyes and ear's witness. For two hours they have enjoyed a blend of classical and classic jazz music. They have journeyed through highs and lows on a musical scale created within the mind of Navarro.

Now the show has ended. The ending piece just as vibrant as the first brings the full range of emotion to a close. The audience has experienced and shared in the emotion of the one who has created the work.

Finished Navarro rises from behind the piano to a roaring applause seeming to last forever. He takes a bow before walking off stage to be greeted by Paris. The huge smile on her face is confirmation that he has done a good job. As he approaches her there is something noticeably wrong with him. Navarro runs to Paris to wrap his arms around her. Though it doesn't feel like a he's hugging her its as if he is resting on her shoulders.

"That was wonderful baby." Paris says. Navarro holds on to her for a second then suddenly his body goes limp as he nearly falls to the floor.

Paris immediately calls for help knowing something is seriously wrong. She struggles to hold him up, as his limp body creates a heavy load for her to bear.

She screams out for help. "Someone help me!" she yells loudly at anyone who will listen. "Navarro baby what's wrong?" she asks as she tries to prop him up against the wall. Navarro tries to speak but before he can utter a word he blacks out. Paris growing more worried screams once more for help. Hoping any near will come to her aid she frantically tries to wake him, shaking his body gently as to not harm him. Those who are standing around watching come running to assist her. After a few seconds there is a crowd of dozens standing around offering help. Paris speaks to Navarro trying to wake him, though her attempts go unanswered.

30

The Sound of Rain

THE SOUND OF RAIN slowly thumps against the windowpane. Softly they create a pattern, a gentle sound sweet and calming to the ear. Navarro's eyes slowly open to see the beautiful face of Paris gleaming over him. She smiles with delight to see that he is awake. She strokes his head and speaks to him. "Hi sleepy head." she says hovering over him.

Navarro tries to sit up in bed but with very little effort, as his body is weak. He slowly tries to gain the strength to speak. "Where am I?" he asks looking at his surroundings, as they are unfamiliar to him.

Paris takes a moment to answer. "You're in the hospital baby."

He senses that she is holding back her emotions. "What happened?" he asks.

She continues to stoke his head trying to keep him still and calm.

"You don't remember?" she asks. Navarro tries to recall the events that took place but can only remember being on stage. It's as if his memory has been wiped of everything after he blacked out. "I remember the stage." he recalls.

"Your show was wonderful people are still talking about it." she informs him. Navarro notices something isn't right. There's something she's not telling him. There's something missing in her words.

"How long?" he asks. Paris looks at him as if she doesn't understand the question. Navarro looks at her and asks again. "How long have I been out of it?"

Paris takes a moment to answer. She strokes his head and searches herself to find the right words to say. "It's been four days."

Navarro sinks deeper into the bed and leans his head back. He doesn't say a word he just lays there. Paris tries to shift his mind to other thoughts.

"Everybody came by to see you." she tells him. Unresponsive to what she has just said he interrupts her. "What's wrong with me?" he asks.

The question Paris knew was coming though she was trying to avoid. She stops stroking his head and places her hand on his chest. He knows that she is holding back so he asks again. "What's wrong with me? Just tell me."

Paris takes a breath before explaining. "The doctor says you have a tumor." He senses the hesitation in her voice. News she doesn't want to give him.

Navarro stares up at the ceiling showing no emotion. After a moment of silence, he asks. "Where?"

Paris takes a breath before speaking. "It's in your brain baby."

The news is like 100 pounds weighing heavy on Navarro's chest. His eyes roll back in his head as he exhales slowly. Paris, searching for a way to make light of the situation tries to comfort him. "But the doctors say it's going to be okay."

Navarro opens his eyes as she speaks to him. Paris trying to hold fast to her emotions can no longer hide the pain she is feeling inside as she begins to cry.

"Baby I'm scared. I thought I was going to lose you" She tells him.

Navarro motions for her to come closer. As she does, he pulls her down to him and places her head on his chest.

"It's okay. I'm going to be okay" he tells her, trying to comfort her as well as building strength for himself. Paris feeling comfort in the words he has just said to her grabs hold of him tightly and lies next to him frozen as if time has stood still.

Navarro kisses her forehead and wraps his arms around her tightly. He lays his head back into his pillow and turns to gaze at the rain falling against the window seal. The two of them lay there feeling safe within each other's arms. They exchange "I love you's" before closing their eyes to rest together. They lay in each other's arms. They lie in silence. Paris feels the strength of Navarro's arms and embrace, something she has not felt in the past four days.

Navarro takes the news unusually well. So many things that have happened in his life have prepared him for possibly the hardest fight he will have yet. He looks to the ceiling and says a prayer to himself. He calls out to God for answers, not for himself, but for Paris. He thinks not of his well being, but of hers as he knows what it is like to feel helpless when those you love got through struggles and there's nothing you can do to help them. Now it is not about him. To Navarro Paris is all that matters now.

31

Full Circle

LIFE HAS COME FULL CIRCLE for Navarro. Love, lose, happiness and pain have consumed his life from birth and now he must find a way to deal with it all coupled with his own illness. Paris has taken Navarro back home. They reach the front door and Navarro enters. Navarro stands in the doorway of his grandfather's house, almost afraid to fully enter. He gazes over the mess he created in his fit of rage. The mess created symbolic of his life's struggles and the chaos encompassed within it.

Behind him in walks Paris. She stands strong giving him support. She places her hand on his shoulder. "Are you okay?" she asks. He turns to her and smiles. "Yes, I'm okay."

Paris walks into the center of the room and surveys the mess.

"Well are you ready to clean up?" she asks him.

Navarro walks to the center and looks around as well. From left to right he looks over the damage he caused. He then turns to her and smiles. "Yes, I think I am."

Navarro takes a deep breath. Facing his past and present in front of him he begins to put things in order. With each piece of broken glass that he picks up, it's like putting together a piece of himself needed to move forward.

After moving from room to room taking hours to put everything back in order they are finished. The two of them stand in the hallway of Delray's home staring at the portraits on the wall. Navarro stands with Paris looking over his shoulder. In his hands he holds the last picture that needs to be placed back on the wall. It's a photo of his grandfather framed in a simple wooden frame.

Paris looks over Navarro's shoulder and comments on the picture. "He looks so young in that photo" she say's. Navarro moves his fingers across the picture.

"Yeah he told me he took this after he played with Miles Davis. I didn't believe him at first." he says with a chuckle and a smile.

Navarro pauses for a moment to look once more before putting the picture in place on the wall. The final piece in place, Navarro exhales as if to say it is finally over. All the pain and frustrations of his past and losses he has endured have now come to an end. Finally, he has found a way to confront and deal with them. No longer allowing them to control him.

After the photo is hung Navarro stands and gives way to a slight smile as Paris wraps her arms around him, kissing him on the cheek. "Come on let's go" she says leading him out of the hall toward the back bedroom. The night has drawn long and the two of them are tired. They both lay down to go to sleep.

As hours pass the house goes quiet again. The two lay asleep both in their own dream world. Finding it hard to have a peaceful sleep, Navarro is visited again by his past. On this night his mother returns to him, as he lies asleep in bed.

She calls to him over and over this dream seems so close to reality. He sees his mother holding him as a child explaining her love for him and her wanting him to move on. Confirmation that what happened in the past was not his fault. He was everything to her and the mistakes she made were not a reflection of how she felt about him. He watches as she holds this younger version of himself all he can do is shed a tear and smile. He reaches out to her and just as she came to him soon, she vanishes.

He awakes to the sounds of rain and the light crashing of thunder. Often, he awakes from his dreams, though this time it's different. The haunting feeling is over. For once he now feels full where he was once empty. He sits up in his bed and looks over at Paris lying asleep next to him. No longer feeling alone he feels lucky, lucky to have her in his life lucky to have her next to him.

He stares at her for a moment before leaning over and kissing her forehead. As he kisses her, she moves closer, reaching for him. Navarro smiles and for a moment sees a future brighter than any day in his past. Unable to sleep he gets out of bed and walks to the study. He makes his way down the cold and drafty hallway until he reaches the doorway. He walks over to the piano and takes a seat. He places his hands across the piano and gently begins to play. As he plays, he takes a few sheets of paper and begins to write down the notes as they come to him. He works through the night on a beautiful piece of work. Slow in pace, romantic in essence. It's a melody rich in emotion that takes hold of your heart as if to squeeze but just a gentle grasp enough to keep your ear.

As he plays tears begin to roll down his face. He closes his eyes and thinks of the past and his future devoid of those who have helped him to become the man he has now grown to be. His feelings seep through the tips of his fingers finding their way to keys beneath them. Although he often creates out of pain, this time it is joy that finds his inspiration. Not a somber tune, but one that is happy and upbeat, a celebration of life.

Suddenly it is over. The playing stops and Navarro sits there with his eyes closed, breathing heavy but slowly. With tears gently rolling down his face he opens his eyes and begins to focus. He looks down at the composition sitting on the piano.

He picks it up and gently places a kiss against the paper. A kiss meant for his mother, his grandfather, and the joy they brought to his life.

He places the composition to his chest and raises his head to the sky. Closing his eyes, he wraps his arms around the piece hugging it as if it were the body of his mother and grandfather. The hug lasts only a moment before he comes down from his emotional high and places his head on the edge of the piano to rest. Finally, he has learned to let go.

32

The Sun Has Risen

A NEW DAY BEGINS AS THE SUN HAS RISEN.
Navarro stands over Paris, as she lies asleep in bed. He kneels
down to kiss her and gently wakes her. As he does, her eyes open
and she smiles. Her smile is brighter than the sun shining through
the bedroom window. She reaches out to him. "Good morning
baby" she says grinning ear to ear.

He takes his hand and moves the hair from her face. "Good
morning beautiful." he says to reply then gently kisses her on her
lips. He looks at her for a moment then gently strokes her hair with
his hand. "I love you." he says to her before heading out of the
room.

"Wait!" she says trying to stop him. "Where are you going?" she asks. Navarro turns back to her and smiles.

"I'm going to take a shower baby. Breakfast is on the table. I'll be back." he says to her before walking out of the room.

Paris rolls over in bed to lie on her back. She sits up in bed then yells out to him. "Okay I love you too".

She takes a moment to gather herself before getting out of bed. She looks over at the window as the sun gleams brighter than it ever has before through Navarro's bedroom window. The light glows against her face as she feels its warmth she begins to smile.

The smell of breakfast in the air entices Paris to get out of bed. She jumps from the bed and walks out into the hallway making her way to the kitchen. Passing the bathroom, she hears the sound of water flowing as Navarro is in there taking a shower. Paris sits down at the table and takes a piece of toast from a saucer.

She sits about to begin eating before thinking to herself she'd like to wait for Navarro to join her. She begins to call out to him, "Navarro, hurry up baby. I'm waiting on you." After a few moments she calls to him again. "Navarro." She waits a few more moments and still no answer.

Growing impatient she gets up from the table and heads toward the bathroom. She walks down the hallway leading to the bathroom the sound of the shower is all she hears.

Getting a little worried she calls to Navarro again. "Navarro, baby can you hear me?" she say's.

The closer she gets to the bathroom all she hears is water running. Her heart begins to pound as she reaches the door. Once there she knocks. She knocks loud enough so that the sound of the shower doesn't drown out the sound of her knocking. She tries to compose herself while calling out to Navarro. "Baby open the door." she yells from the other side.

"Can you hear me?" she asks. No answer still, she becomes even more worried. She reaches down to grab the doorknob. Turning it, she notices the door is open. She slowly goes in calling to Navarro once more.

"Baby I'm coming in can you hear me?" she say's moving slowly toward the shower. She walks through the steam filled room staring at the shower she doesn't see a figure in there at all.

She walks over to the drawn curtain and pulls it back slowly. As she pulls the curtain back, she is devastated by what she sees. She falls to the floor on her knees crying as she sees Navarro's lifeless body lying on the shower floor. She reaches into the shower and grabs his body cradling him and crying out to him. She shakes him gently to try to wake him. There is a small trickle of blood coming from his head and nose possibly as a result of fainting in the shower.

She continues to try to wake him, but gets no response. She grows even more worried as he is not breathing. No sign of a pulse, no breath, as he lies limp in her arms. Alas her efforts are of no use for she knows he is dead. She holds him rocking back and forth holding his head close to her body as she weeps. Comforting him even still long after the life has left his body. She holds him as if to protect him. Protect him from anything else that will come to try to harm him. Protect him even from the drops of water that rain down on the two of them from the shower.

Amidst the pain she feels she takes solace in knowing that Navarro can finally rest at peace. She looks up to the heavens and screams out in pain. Through the sound of water crashing against the tub the sound of her pain echoes against the bathroom walls. Helpless she just holds him close to her not wanting to let him go.

33

A Familiar Sound

A FAMILIAR SOUND PLAYS filling the air. The cold of winter one-year later has come again. Though the cold outside does not disturb the warm feeling trapped within the apartment of Paris.

The flow of traffic is drowned out by the sound of a piano playing. Sitting at her window holding a cup of coffee Paris stares out into the evening sky. Even the sound of a bird's song cannot penetrate through the sound of music playing in her apartment.

The sound very familiar, it's the sound of Navarro playing the piano. Paris sits listening to a composition of Navarro's, while staring out of the window reminiscing on time past and the feeling of what Navarro gave to her and what they shared together.

She sits as the sun shines through her window creating a glow as beautiful as the sound levitating through the air around her. She takes a sip of her coffee then looks down to something in her hand. Her eyes survey a flyer advertising a need for dancers for an upcoming play. As all things will have their day, a second chance at living out her dream has come full circle. She sound of Navarro is confirmation that he approves of this move. He would want her to continue her pursuit of her dream.

Suddenly her attention is drawn to something in the corner of her eye. She slowly turns to look down at the floor. She gives way to a subtle smile. Though subtle it is as warm and bright as the sun. Soon the object of attention comes into view.

Paris sits still brandishing a loving smile as she stares at a beautiful baby boy sitting on the floor playing with one of his toys, a small little piano. The child looks up and reaches out to her, to his mother. Paris' smile gives light that Navarro's spirit will always be with her, through the everlasting sound of his music and the son they've created together, a son that carries the look of both of them within his eyes and his small beautiful face.

Paris knows that her soul and that of Navarro will always be intertwined forever in time as this too was meant to be. Knowing that in life there will be many twists and turns along the journey. There will always be a light at the end of the tunnel. Even when all is dark and lost, through it all something beautiful will remain.

So, at last, Love's Epiphany has come to pass....

Thanks….

Thank God for the sun
Thank God for my mother
Thank God for the moon
Thank God for my grandmother
Thank God for the rain
Thank God for my brother, sister, family, and friends
Thank God for inspiration

I Thank God.

NAVARIA
ENTERPRIZES

NAVARIA ENTERPRISES

Navaria Productions
Copyright © 2021 Navaria Enterprises
Registered, WGAw No. 2106464

The Words
Of
Loves Epiphany

Just Another Day

(Navarro Love)

I remember a day with less trouble
A day with less strife
I remember life without sorrow
I remember life

Is it possible to live a life devoid of drama?
Is it possible to live in a world?
with a more compassionate form of karma
Life has its up and downs,
But I never thought those ups would never come around

Is it possible to tell the good days from bad?
When the good days were just as bad as the last
Is there light within the dark?
Praying for a flicker, just a spark

If its one thing I know for sure
the days they will come and go
Each day I awake hoping purpose has been revealed to me
What am I here for, what am I meant to be?

So, until that dream has come to pass
And truth has come at long last
Asking God please if I may
Grant me just another day

Contact Us

NavariaEnterprises@gmail.com

For More Information and Available

Titles From

Navarro Love

www.ingramcontent.com/pod-product-compliance
Lightning Source LLC
Chambersburg PA
CBHW072235170626
46813CB00003B/1240